Finding Our Missing Peace

Michelle Vereen

ISBN: 1-4701-3883-2
ISBN-13: 9781470138837

Dedication

This book is dedicated to two wonderful women who helped me find my missing peace through our laughter and tears, good food and Belinis (especially the Belinis)! May peace always be with you my special friends~

Chapter 1

It's Saturday, April 3rd. The first Saturday of the new month and we know what that means! Girls night out. This was our time—time that stood still with no interruptions, no hassling husbands, and no whiny kids; the time when three very beautiful, very busy career women came together and shared drinks, laughter, sorrows and everything in between. Our special gathering place is a quaint little Italian restaurant in the middle of town where we would each drive equal distances to meet. Sure the food is delicious, but the best part of our special meeting place is for the drinks. We had found no other place that served **THE BEST** and I mean **THE BEST** Italian frozen mixed Belinis.

My name is Brooke Anderson and some people may be able to relate to my story. Maybe not. My two best friends are Ellie Thomas and Madison Mc-Dowell. Although we come from different worlds we seem to fit like peanut butter and jelly. No, if you are a woman reading this you could better understand our relationship if I told you we fit together like peanut butter and chocolate. My favorite combination of all times! We are quite different from each other and we have been told that on a number of occasions, but there is a force that brings us together and leads our spirits to Angelina's Fine Italian Restaurant- like clockwork the first Saturday of each new month.

Ellie, the hopeless romantic that puts her heart on the line and trusts with all she has finds that it seems to always burn her in the end. A single divorced woman, with two beautiful children, who is gorgeous but doesn't see it. Her heart is made of gold and this touches everyone around her. She is the girl that listens with a strong ear while her weak heart breaks. Ellie teaches young children because that is what fate handed her. Her parents made this known to her at a very early age. That was their career choice so of course it would be hers too. Teaching, they told her, was in her blood. She accepted this fate, but at a cost. The cost was her dream not being fulfilled. No, teaching was not her dream career. Her dreams ran much deeper than wiping runny noses and teaching the sounds of letters. A computer analyst is what her dreams center around. This is the intriguing personality that draws me to her mainly due to the fact that technology just doesn't make any sense to me.

Madison, the youngest of our group, doesn't seem to care what people think and shows no weakness. Sure her heart has been broken by a man that doesn't know what commitment is if it stood up and slapped him in the face, but somehow she has gotten over the fact that Seth (her ex. boyfriend, lover.....) no longer has ties to her or their young son James. Ellie and I have never seen tears shed and wonder how Madison can talk about the painful things she and her son have been through without releasing one lonesome tear. To me, that is strength at its best!

Now her degree wasn't an easy one to obtain. Chemistry/Forensic Science was the degree she set her mind to and accomplished. Ellie and I admire her because of the potential and intelligence Madison displays. With the terrible downturn of the economy being at an all time high, her position as a researcher with a well know company is on the rocks. Her stress now is weighing on her like a ton of bricks. Without her top pay and no support from deadbeat Seth how will she and her son make it?

Then there is me. I'm not the super bright one like Madison, nor am I the soft hearted giver like Ellie. I am the over dramatic crazy girl that swears that I am who I am because of my zodiac sign. I do find humor in places where some can't or don't and sometimes this scares people away and sometime it pulls others closer to me. I am a teacher also. But like Ellie, I have dreams too. My dream is to be an actress and show the world that I have talent and can be someone else, someone who may not be so predictable. Now my two best friends think I have the world at my feet. They think this because I am the only married one in our group. I tell them life is never what it seems especially when you are on the outside looking in. Life with three teenage daughters and a husband that struggles to make it in his career isn't what I call an envied life. Our struggles are similar, but different. We have proven to one another that the strength from each of us provides what we need to make it in our separate worlds.

It's 3:30 p.m. and we know it's time to high step it so we arrive on time to our destination. David, my wonderful husband of twenty long devoted years is telling me I look hot, but I, not believing him (due to the fact that I've added 20 extra pounds to my life since college) continue to try to find humor in my negative thoughts. I curse as I try to button the wrinkle free khaki pants I just recently purchased, but tell my unbelieving husband that I've had these pants for years and just found them in our unorganized closet. Same lie I tell each time I make a new purchase. But I know that my husband knows they're new because the look on his face reveals it. A look I've learned quite well. I tell David I don't know what he sees in me that he thinks is so hot as he looks at me with that dreamy look in his eyes (with total admiration) that's been there all along. He laughs and knows it's a losing battle to try to explain it to such a thick headed woman. I comb through my damp, straight, fine hair that I loathe and apply a fresh coat of light pink lipstick to my pouty lips, grab my keys, tell my family good-bye and head out to my car. I just can't wait for this much needed girl time.

Meanwhile, Ellie who is 20 miles south of me, is struggling to get ready and feed her children their favorite meal of chicken nuggets and skinny french fries (that's what her children named them) with a load of ketchup and honey mustard sauce on the side, a scrumptious meal to please any five and seven year old. The babysitter seems to be late again and she thinks to herself when am I going to find someone who can be a little more dependable? Her next thought being how am I going to straighten this crazy, out of control fuzz ball that rests on my head? She looks at the clock even though she tells herself not to and realizes she is to be at Angelina's in 30 minutes! She is well aware of the looks she will receive from Madison and Brooke when she shows up 20 maybe 30 minutes fashionably late. Why could they always make it on time and she couldn't? Why did her mind always have to wander and lead her to those glances of discontent? Then she realizes that she is no different than the babysitter that she has been cursing in her mind. Hmm...I wonder if this is how my friends feel about me all the times I show up late. As these thoughts are streaming through her mind, she realizes that she has in fact lost 5 more minutes.

Katie Lynn and Hunter settle down at the bar in their kitchen ready to munch away on this much favored meal. Ellie kisses them and tells them that mommy has to get a shower and to not open the door if the bell rings. A rule that has been drilled in their heads since they were old enough to understand. As she makes her way up the winding staircase to her master bedroom, she thinks to herself—Oh why did I choose to live in a 2 story house and why can't I be in shape to climb these stupid stairs faster! As much as she would like those creepy, negative thoughts to leave they just won't. As she enters her cluttered bedroom the same dreaded memories begin to overtake her. Memories that included a husband that no longer would be. These memories poking her to find a reason why her husband Jason, of 9 years, had to leave her. Why did he have to leave this beautiful house, and his beautiful children? These questions constantly burn through her like molten lava from a spewing volcano. Do the negative thoughts that she harbors come from that miserable day that he told her that their life together could no longer be? Maybe, possibly, definitely! She thinks to herself, that those thoughts must be pushed aside because in a short time she will be with the girls that bring her the most joy she always looks forward to on the first Saturday of each new month.

Madison busily helps her son James clean up his toys, science investigation kits, and video games so she can leave her home without worrying about the scattered mess that lies in their four bedroom house. This was a house that was bought some time back in hopes that she and Seth would have more children. But she too, like Ellie, had to face the fact that Seth was never returning to the place they once called their dream home. Thoughts of how she arrived at this place in her life were etched deeply in her soul. These thoughts never seemed to quit churning in her mind. How could she, who came from a hard working Irish middle class family with such determination of never giving up, endlessly studying, having no social life and graduating at the top of her class be at this dead end? Of course she would never let on that she, the one her friends depended on for strength, actually did worry constantly about how her 8 year old son feels about having an absent father and constantly fearing that the wonderful job she has today may not be hers tomorrow. Why she was human too. No, she will tediously do what she has trained herself to do time and again and that is to move forward and dig another grave in her head to dump those dreadful thoughts. No tight holds could or would be put on her. No, siree! She is strong and damn it she will continue tc be not only for her own sanity but also for her son.

James grandparents were coming to babysit him. James hated the word babysit because he didn't consider himself a baby anymore. His 9th birthday was in a few months so he told his mom that he preferred the word company instead. So Madison made sure this time to tell James that his company was coming soon to visit him. That seemed to please him. Better thoughts found their way to Madison as she knew her parents would arrive at any minute and her smile began to find its way to her attractive, young face. She pulled her long, shiny auburn hair away from her shoulders and tied it in a low ponytail. This was her signature look on any given day.

James had so looked forward to spending the evening with his grand-parents, especially his grandpa who was the only positive male influence in his life these days. Grandpa knew just the right things to say to James and somehow always made him feel important. James' own father didn't seem to know how to do that and it was such a shame. Seth chose to make a life for himself minus his flesh and blood and this new life included a much younger girl. Madison didn't think this new person could even earn the rights be called a woman, this due to the fact that she was only 22 years of age. This girl was barely through her teenage years and didn't have any business be-coming Seth's wife. What the hell was he thinking? Obviously he wasn't. As the thoughts crept slowly back, as they seem to do quite often, Madison heard a knock at the door.

"Grandpa, grandpa!" These were the happy words that came from the best part of her life. And was she always happy to see the excitement illumi-nate from her beautiful son.

Chapter 2

Angelina's was busier than usual. With spring break approaching it always seemed to bring people out of hibernation and into the delectable smells that permeated through the restaurant. Angelina's became our spot somewhat by accident. Last year the three of us were trying to decide where to eat lunch. We decided to meet at a small, but well known burger joint that happened to be located next door to Angelina's. When we had arrived we found to our surprise that Eddie's Burgers was no longer in business. We later learned that Eddie, a man of mystery, had left town one day without anyone knowing where he went and why he left. Rumors spread like wildfire and no one knew what to believe. Some say he had been tied up with the Mafia and there had been a hit out on him. Others claimed he changed his identity and faked his own death to escape a terrible divorce that would probably force him to declare bankruptcy and cause him be left with nothing. Eddie's sat empty and all we could do was stare and speculate. It was Madison who pulled us from our trance and asked us if we were in the mood for Italian. Ellie and I both shook our heads at the same time and that is how our tradition began.

Tonight, I was the first of us to arrive at the restaurant and soon noticed that Madison, with her glowing young face, was approaching the door of Angelina's. When she saw me, she opened her mouth to speak and I answered the question that was on the tip of her tongue. "Yes, I have already put my name on the waiting list." Madison laughed and she told me I always seem to know what she's going to say before she says it. My spirit had already begun to lift. I, like Madison and Ellie could not wait to slurp down the fruity Belinis that waited before us and to take the first bite of the scrumptious fine Italian food that made our mouths water for more. "How have you been Brooke?" Madison asked. I stated that I had been very busy and couldn't wait to sit down and hold a decent conversation with my besties minus the interruptions. The next thing she said was, "Late again?" We both laughed and

I knew who she was referring to. We waited for ten minutes and then the beeper the hostess gave us began flashing. We made sure to let the hostess know that there was one more person joining us before she took us to our booth.

Our booth was in a cozy little corner and Madison and I were both glad about that. When the three of us got together we always tended to get a little louder, so out of respect for the other customers we felt this booth was the perfect place for us. We definitely didn't want management to ask us to leave either. As we patiently waited for Ellie to arrive we made small talk until our waitress made her way over to our table. She was one of their best waitresses and this made us happy to know that our service would be top notch. She smiled at us and said she was happy to see that we made our way back to Angelina's and then asked us what we would like to drink. Without delay, Madison and I, in unison, said, " Belini!" The waitress thought we had rehearsed that but we told her we had looked forward to that drink all month. She laughed and said, " Two delicious Belinis coming right up." Madison ordered one more for Ellie and we both hoped she would be arriving any minute. I wanted to know how things had been lately with Madison and James so I asked her if anything new had happened since the last time we talked. "Well, Seth has completely stopped all communication with James and me. He won't answer our calls, won't return them and doesn't even bother to text us. For all I know he could be dead." I said, "Would that be so bad?" "Brooke, that's an awful thing for you to say, but you may have a point," she said. I looked at her with such sadness and couldn't stop wondering how a father (if he even remotely had the rights to hold that title) could completely end all communication with his son. "The last time I spoke with him was two and a half weeks ago and he had told me then that work had picked up so much that he barely had time to eat and that is why time had lapsed between phone calls and text messages." I told her it may be time for her and her adorable son to cut all ties with Seth. She replied, "I can't bring myself to do that with James being so young and all." Oh boy was all I could say to myself. As the conversation came to a halt, I looked up and happened to notice Ellie walking toward our table.

Ellie seemed to walk with a little more pep in her step while her gorgeous, long brown hair glistened in the soft light. Her warm smile made me think that anyone who left her could surely not be in their right mind. Ellie seemed relaxed and happy for once and I wondered what had brought this about. Could it be that she was just so excited to soon be joining her two most favorite people in the whole world or was it something else? The suspense was killing me! As she got even closer to our table, Madison and I could see her glowing and we knew we had to find out what new change had occurred in her life. Before Ellie could sit down, Jessica (our waitress) had appeared with our drinks and it made Ellie smile to know that Madison and I had not forgotten her as she spotted the three delicious Belinis that were balanced oh so carefully on the small tray that Jessica had skillfully carried on one hand.

When Jessica placed the last Belini on our table we all began talking at once. Yes, it was official! Our gathering was getting underway. As I sipped, quicker than the others, I knew I couldn't wait any longer. "Ellie, why are you glowing?" I asked. She nervously laughed and said, "Well, something wonderful has happened since the last time we all met and I do want you all to be the first ones to know my good news." Oh how this raised Madison's and my suspicions. Madison blurted out, "Who's the guy?" I cracked up at the spontaneity of Madison's question. I was in complete shock because up to this point Ellie hadn't mentioned anything about a new someone in her life. As far as I knew she was still in the mourning stage of her ended marriage. A marriage that ended abruptly one year and one month ago to be exact when Jason left Ellie and their children with no remorse at all. We eagerly waited for Ellie to quit sipping her berry flavored Belini to continue the conversation that kept us on edge, but Jessica was walking toward our table ready to take our order. Were we ready to order? We should have been because we three seem to be creatures of habit at this place. Ellie told the waitress that we needed a few more minutes. Maybe change was what Ellie needed. Heck, I couldn't even think about ordering because I was too anxious to find out who this new man could be in my best friends life. Being bold was a gift I felt I had been blessed with so I used my gift and blurted out, "Well Ellie, who is it already?" She looked up from her menu, blushing and began telling us about a fascinating man she had met just the week before. I gave her a strange look and wondered why she had not mentioned him in our past conversations. Obviously she didn't read my expression because she continued her story adding the details that she knew would have us hanging on to every word. Madison, with that analytical mind of hers, wanted to know specifics while I still wanted to know how and why she kept this from us for a whole week! As questions flew Ellie's way, we knew we should glance at the menu quickly before Jessica came back to take our order. But hell weren't we going to order what we always ordered? Ellie kept us hanging on edge by telling us to focus on ordering and that after we placed our orders she would continue her story.

Jessica made her way back to our table and we, Madison and I, couldn't order fast enough. We couldn't wait to hear what Ellie had to tell us. What sad people we had become. Our lives obviously were so boring that we had to rely on Ellie for much needed drama. As our waitress had jotted down the last item to be ordered, I couldn't wait any longer. "Okay continue on," I squealed. "Well, as I said before, I met a fascinating man and his name is Michael. He is a little older than me and tells me he is a self made man. I don't know what he looks like yet though." Before I could pop out a reply, Madison wanted to know how Ellie could be seeing a guy whom she had never seen before. Before Ellie could answer that question Madison said, "Oh no! Please tell me you didn't meet him online!" By the look on Ellie's face Madison already knew the answer to the previous question asked. "Now Ellie, I have told you a hundred times before that it's not safe to meet and fall for someone online." Ellie assured Madison and me that he was an amazing guy who made a decent living and was single. His excuse for not being in a committed relationship in the past is due to all the time he spent in building his business. This he told her was something that he wanted to change. He was ready for a meaningful relationship. Judging by Madison's expression I could tell she wasn't buying what this new guy was selling. I too, had questions that I wasn't sure if I should ask. The main question I had was, Could this guy be a professional player? I didn't dare ask her this, but boy did I want to. Ellie told us she knew what we were thinking, but she believed in her heart that Michael was the answer to her daily prayers. I was at a loss for words and I gave Madison a look that spoke volumes.

It grew very quiet at our table and that seemed to be the first time that has ever happened. Where did my drink go? I thought as I sipped the last bit of crushed berries at the bottom of my glass. I then began watching as our glasses perspired and thought about the beads of water and how they slowly trickled down just as Ellie's tears had done the night Jason left. I got an empty feeling in my stomach that had nothing to do with hunger. The what- ifs began crowding my thoughts. What if she falls hard for this new mystery man and he disappoints her? What if he's a murderer? What if he is married? Any of these could be possible. Couldn't they? As I struggled with these thoughts I decided to be the one to change the subject. Ellie wouldn't allow that though. She interrupted me and continued the conversation that had been quickly ended. "Anyway, Michael seems so different than any man I have ever been interested in," continued Ellie. Madison rolled her eyes and Ellie noticed but chose to ignore it. Okay, so maybe this is what she needs to get back into the dating world; a nice guy who will treat her well. After all, this could bring back the fun and happiness she was missing. But who was I kidding? Madison and I both knew that when Ellie fell, she fell hard. Ellie herself knew that even if she refused to admit it.

The conversation came to an end and it had grown too quiet in our little corner booth. Where was the laughter that we had shared so many times before? Madison changed the subject by telling us that Seth had ended (or said he had) the relationship that he was having with that tramp he had been spending all of his time with. I asked her how she knew this and she said word travels fast. I wondered if this meant that he was going to slowly try to creep back into her life or was he going to move on to the next best thing. That guy played too many games and Madison knew that, but sometimes she would let her vulnerability get in the way and forgive him only to be burned again and again. Ellie wanted to say something, but kept quiet for now.

It had seemed like so many things had taken place since the last time we had all been together. Madison and Ellie didn't find it too surprising that my life seemed to stay somewhat constant. Ellie gave Madison an accusing look and I could feel the tension building. Madison knew why the darts were being thrown her way, but chose to ignore them. "Well well it looks like Madison doesn't know how to let go," said Ellie. Oh no this conversation just won't die. These words seemed to seethe out of Ellie's mouth and if those words could be captured by the human hand they would burn right through the skin. Madison knew she couldn't ignore that comment. I wanted all this tension to stop, but somehow it had gotten way out of my control. My drink had been long gone and I was at a loss for words. Before anyone could say another word our delicious smelling entrees had arrived at our table. Ellie and Madison seemed to still be stewing, but not me. I couldn't wait to please my taste buds.

The aromas from our meals were simply amazing. Madison ordered the Rotini (her favorite) and Ellie's choice was the five layered lasagna. I admired the fetuchini alfredo dish that had been placed so gently in front of me. I could eat this meal every day. To break the silence I commented on how everything looked so delicious and Ellie, looking at her empty glass, asked the waitress for another Belini. The knife Ellie used to cut through her lasagna could have been the same knife used to cut through the silence at our table. No other time had I known it to be so awkward as to this moment with my two best friends. No one at our table seemed to even make comments about the food. We always took turns making comments about our meals. This time that wasn't going to happen. I couldn't take it anymore so I totally changed the subject. The silence was too much for me. I began a whole new conversation that centered around me. I told them that I had really been considering breaking into acting and thought about auditioning with a small theater on the other side of town. They seemed happy for me but I didn't see the enthusiasm that I thought they could at least fake for my sake.

Madison quickly ate her Rotini and made the excuse that she had to get back home because her parents couldn't watch James all night. I knew that simply wasn't the truth, but I left it alone and didn't dare let on that I doubted her. We exchanged our good byes and it really bothered me that this evening, that we had longed for, was ending on such a sour note.

As Ellie and I sat there in silence, finishing our meals, I felt that I needed to initiate a brief conversation about the heated disagreement that had taken place a short time ago. I don't know why silence always seemed to bother me. "Ellie, you know Madison and I love you like a sister and we just don't want you going through hell again." I wasn't sure how she would respond to my comment so I gave her a very gentle smile and wished I would have ordered a second Belini. As I looked at her carefully, I noticed the one lonesome tear that was slowly trickling down from her sparkling brown eye. As she went to speak, silence seemed to grab her words. She figured that whatever it was she was about to say may be discounted by me. Instead she took my hand and gently squeezed it. At this point I knew then that we all had so much to learn from each other.

Chapter ?

way of cours
Madison
but wh
it wo
m

When I returned home I noticed that David had left a kitchen table explaining that he went out with Tom (his best friend) and would be home later. This was no surprise at all. Besides spending much of his free time with his daughters and me, he seemed to equally spend time with Tom. They had become very good friends over the two years they have known each other and I was glad that he had found a person that seemed to be so much like him. The house was much too quiet with David and the girls not being there. Everyone seemed to always have such varied agendas anymore. The girls had their freedom to come and go as they pleased now that they were all old enough to drive and have jobs.

Lost in my thoughts, I decided to lie down and relax for a while. This evening's events sure stressed me out and made me very tired. As I walked into our bedroom I noticed the computer had been left on. Strange, I thought. David always shut down the computer before he ever left the house. His OCD made sure of that, but for some odd reason that wasn't the case this time. Oh well it wouldn't kill me to get up and shut it down. So I pulled myself up from the bed and went to the computer. As I tapped the space bar to bring light to the screen I noticed a message that had popped up. Probably a message intended for one of the girls. Anyway, my curiosity got the best of me so I clicked on the message. I read the message that said, I can't wait to see you! It was signed XOXO. How sweet it was to be young and in love I thought. This was a message that was solely intended for one of our lucky daughters. This made me smile and I was happy to know that my mood had lightened. Although the night had not gone as planned somehow I had known that everything was going to be just fine.

Across town Madison was making James his favorite dessert and trying to push this evening's events out of her mind. Chocolate ice cream, chocolate syrup, whip cream and sprinkles is what James was demanding in a polite

. This had been his favorite dessert since he was just a tot. Yes, new feeding him this sugary mess would hype him to no end, cares it was still early enough in the evening that she didn't think ld affect him getting to sleep later. She figured his sugary high would llow before bedtime. He was all she had and she was going to do her best to keep him her little man as long as she could! As she added a few more sprinkles to the sugary concoction she heard her cell phone ring. She grabbed it and noticed that Brooke was the caller. She decided not to take the call. Who wanted to recap this evening's drama? She didn't. Besides why would either of them call her when they knew she was still brewing. She handed James his sweet dessert and delighted in watching him take the first bite.

"Hello, beautiful!" Ellie blushed as her new good looking, slightly older gentleman greeted her. Michael and Ellie had decided that going to Starbucks for a cappucino would be a great and safe place to meet face to face for the first time. Although it was nearing 8:30 on a Saturday evening, this newly opened Starbucks was jumping. A wonderful location smack dab in the middle of town proved for this place to be a total success. Ellie had butterflies swirling around in her stomach and although it was a bit un-comfortable to feel this way she actually kind of liked it. Happiness began overflowing in her. This happiness had been buried for so long. She couldn't even focus on what Michael was saying. She admired his gentle, gorgeous, blue eyes as they sat facing each other. She knew she would never grow tired looking into those eyes. Her conscience kept telling her at that moment that she could not screw this up and she listened to it carefully. This one, she thought, won't get away!

Ellie knew the extra attention she had put into her make- up, hair and clothing choice was the most important decision she had made in quite some time. Who cares what Madison thought. She was a grown woman, thirty four to be exact and wasn't getting any younger. Ellie slowly began compar-ing Michael to Jason. Why was she allowing her brain to do that? Jason was gone and should have been the faintest memory, but her mind was making him so vivid right now. Both men were very attractive but in such different ways. "So what do you think about that?" "Huh?" was all Ellie could say. Damn she got stuck in that dream world of hers and Michael probably now thinks she is a scatter brained twit. "Oh I am so sorry," replied Ellie. Michael smiled and told her how fine he thought she looked. She giggled, but didn't care if she sounded like a teenager. Men loved that about women. The younger the woman looked and acted the better! She pinched herself to keep from daydreaming and hoped she wouldn't have to do that all night.

As Ellie talked about her childhood through her college days, Michael sat and admired her beauty. He too was having a difficult time staying focused. He was so impressed with this beautiful, vibrant woman and he thought to himself that this was a wonderful time in his life to meet Ellie. He had been longing for something new, refreshing, and well to be honest a slightly younger woman who could make him feel alive again. His fortieth birthday had come and gone leaving him feeling somewhat lost in his life. He knew meeting her was a great way to bring him some happiness that was well deserved. His passion for her was growing strong. He wasn't a young inexperienced man. He would know how to keep her interested without seeming desperate. He wouldn't let on the excitement she was able to bring to him. Showing her that excitement early on could have damaging effects. He didn't want to scare her away and make her think he was only interested in one thing. He would play it cool.

They talked about things they liked and things they disliked. Ellie couldn't believe how compatible they were. The difference in their age didn't seem to matter. Ellie had grown up with older brothers, one the exact age of Michael. Growing up, listening to the music and watching movies from the 1980's were what they found they had the most in common. Michael shared with Ellie his high school memories and she adored the way he reminisced. He told her that he had been an all star baseball player in high school and had promised scholarships to several different well known colleges, but wasn't able to pursue his baseball career. He went on to tell her that during his senior year he had torn his ACL for the second time. This meant no more baseball, no scholarships, and no more dreams of being in the World Series one day. Ellie didn't know what to say. She could see the despair in his eyes as he told her his life loss. She touched his hand and told him how genuinely sorry she was to hear that. "That was a long time ago," he said. Michael began telling her that he decided to live at home and enroll in the community college that happened to be close by. His second dream had been to open a nursery; a nursery that sold plants and trees. His face lit up as he told her that gardening and landscaping had always been his favorite thing to do besides baseball. "If plan A doesn't happen, go to plan B." Ellie admired him for his determination. As she listened to him, Ellie happened to notice that they were the only two customers there and the employees behind the counter had begun their closing time routine. She did not want the night to end. She felt wildly courageous so in her best flirtatious manner, she smiled and flipped her thick hair away from her face and asked Michael if he wanted to come back to her place since Starbucks would soon be closing.

Wow! He couldn't believe she had been so forward, but he didn't mind. He was actually very flattered. He wanted to leave with her and definitely go back to her place. What man wouldn't? He wanted her to know he was interested, but he also knew that it was too early for this. He knew if he went back to her place tonight it wouldn't be any time that he would have her undressed, making passionate love to her, and possibly disrespecting her. Twenty plus years ago he wouldn't have hesitated, but tonight was different. She was different and he did not want to take advantage of her. As they stood up, he leaned over to give her a hug. He whispered in her ear that he had an amazing evening, but had an early day tomorrow. She wasn't disappointed because his words were so gentle and she felt in such a strong way that she could trust him. She loved the way he whispered in her ear.

Michael then backed away and admired her beauty. He told her that she was a breath of fresh air and he couldn't wait to see her again. Electric shocks made their way through Ellie's body and she told him she couldn't wait to see him again.

Self control is the name of the game, Michael told himself over and over as he drove home. He looked at the clock in his truck and couldn't believe that it was already 11:00. It was like time had stood still with Ellie that night. The urges that he had been feeling fifteen minutes earlier, when she had asked him to come back to her place didn't seem to want to go away. His mind knew what self control meant, but the growth in his pants didn't. What he needed right now was to roll the windows down and hope for some nice cool air to wash over him. Who was he kidding? He lived in the south and cool air in the month of April just didn't exist too often.

The phone woke me around 10:00 a.m. Sunday morning. "Oh crap, David! We slept through the alarm clock." The Anderson family had made it a strict habit to be in church every Sunday morning since the girls were little. David, not being an avid church-goer in his younger years, had learned that being in church with his beautiful family was essential. He and Brooke had noticed that as the girls got older, the family seemed to be sliding away from their church attendance. He woke up with dirty thoughts and knew he should be sitting in a church pew right about now.

In his most alluring voice he said, "Brooke sweetie, since we missed church how about you and I have some time together? We do have a little free time before the girls wake up. And it has been a while."

David and I had a great sex life, but lately David seemed to be more stressed than usual. All marriages go through the ebb and flow of life and this was normal. I knew he was ready because I felt the strong, thick growth in his boxers. This always made me hot. He climbed on top and ran his tongue around the inside and outside of my ear. After twenty years, our lovemaking had been pretty good. We had always enjoyed trying new positions and normally did so each time we made love, but this morning seemed a little different. His moves were mechanical, almost robot like. The tenderness wasn't present and a slight trickle of fear swarmed over me. My inner voice told me something wasn't right, but maybe I was just overreacting. As he finished, he jumped up and without a word left me lying there. This was not really his style and I began to wonder what was causing this new behavior. I decided to keep my thoughts to myself and dismissed the negative thinking altogether.

My phone began buzzing again. This time I was ready to answer. It was Ellie on the other end. "Oh Brooke, I had the most amazing night!" Oh goodness- what had she done? Had she given into her desires with the new man in her life? I didn't want to know, but I knew she would tell me anyway. "Ellie, he is my soul mate," she excitedly told me. As I listened to her explain the past night's events I watched David get dressed. He gave me a sexy smile that always turned me to jell-o. I flirted with my eyes as he came to my bedside and rubbed my breast.

He whispered I love you and left the room. Oh, I just wanted so bad for my best friend to have what I had always had. The evening made me feel so good for her and the best part of the conversation was the part when she told me they went their separate ways after their date. Thank you God is what I said to that. She knows I would not approve of a one night stand even if she is single. I told her that this guy sounds like he could be the real deal. Oh how Madison would think Ellie and I were insane. It sounds like this guy wants a meaningful relationship though. I wanted to know when they were to meet again and she told me she didn't know for sure but she thought it would be soon. Before our conversation came to an end, Ellie had invited me to go with her to the Town Center Mall. I told her to give me one hour and I would meet her at her house.

Well, I guess I should have asked David if we had plans, but I got so caught up in Ellie's excitement. I found David in the kitchen making brunch and put my arms around him. "Baby, I'm going shopping with Ellie in a bit." He didn't mind. That's what I loved the most about my husband—he never seemed to put restrictions on me. As I showered, I thanked God for giving me such a caring husband, our wonderful daughters and of course included in my prayer all the other blessings He so richly has given to me. How many people truly have what I do? Despite recent money troubles, I really do have it all. This thought began to scare me though because I know that things can't always be this close to perfect and wondered if there was going to be a day where the devil would step in and take it all away.

As I was driving to Ellie's house I felt a little guilty that Madison wouldn't be included, but I knew that inviting her would only make Ellie angry. She was still stewing about yesterday's comments. I'm sure that today would be devoted to Ellie sharing every last detail about Michael and her night with him. To ease my guilt, I would invite Madison to go somewhere after work with me this week. When I arrived at Ellie's I thought about how much fun it will be to get out and do some shopping since I haven't been in so long. I did manage to save a little money from my check. I pictured a new blouse or shoes that I would like to buy. When Ellie answered the door I automatically noticed how wonderful she looked as she stood there glowing. She told me she was so proud of herself for staying up until 2:00 a.m. cleaning her house. She said she couldn't go to sleep last night and had no interruptions from the kids because Jason had them for the weekend. She was ecstatic to know that she could wake up to an immaculate house. Wish I could have said the same thing about my house. We made small talk and I told her how great her house looked and then we made our way to my car. We loved to shop and couldn't wait to get to the Town Center Mall.

Chapter 4

As we pulled into the Town Center Mall Ellie told me that she wanted to check out the new boutique—Beverly's Boutique. From what I had heard, this boutique was a takeoff of Fredrick's of Hollywood. I slyly looked at Ellie and asked her why she wanted to visit this boutique. With a quirky giggle she said she needed to update her lingerie. In the earlier stages of my marriage I would update my lingerie quite often, but seemed to have stopped doing that about ten years ago. David didn't seem to mind. Ellie must be wanting to find just the right little number that would rock Michael's world. Wow, now I was starting to envy my best friend. The first thing Ellie told me as we walked into Beverly's Boutique was she had thrown away all her sexy nighties soon after Jason left. She couldn't bear to look at them because too many memories came flooding back. I could understand that. I told her it was time to make changes and this place would be the perfect place to start. We both laughed at that. "Brooke, look at this hot little number," she said in her sexiest voice. I told her I knew she would look great in it and it was the perfect color for her. With her tanned skin and dark hair, red was the ultimate color. There wasn't much to it and I thought if this guy Michael hadn't committed, he would after seeing her in this. Ellie crazily pranced around the store as if she was a child that had just been let loose in a candy store. She would grab an item, put it up to her body, pose, grab another item and do it all over again. My head began spinning, but I wasn't going to put a damper on her happiness.

"Brooke, why don't you find yourself something sexy?" I told her that I hadn't planned on spending extra money on lingerie. She said, "Honey don't you think your hubby would go crazy to see you in something naughty?" Obviously she didn't know my David. "David doesn't care about all this sexy, frilly stuff," I said. She looked at me like I had three eyes and horns growing from my head. She then gave me a speech about how all men, even men who had been married for a long time, had expected their wives to dress a certain way in the bedroom. I looked at her in confusion and asked her if that was the case why hadn't he ever said anything to me before. "Men don't have to say anything, Brooke, it's a given." I just agreed because this conversation was beginning to bother me. What if Ellie was right and I was making David settle for a ratty old nightgown that I repeatedly had worn over and over the last ten years or so? What does Ellie know? Not to be ugly and I dared not say a thing to her, but who was the married gal here? Lost in my thoughts, I noticed Ellie had slipped into the dressing room. I decided to sit down on a chair by the window. I somehow knew we would be here a while.

After an hour and a half, Ellie had found the perfect number. She begged for me to come see her in it and I felt a little odd going back there to watch her model the hottest piece she could find. I must be getting old, I thought to myself because for some bizarre reason I didn't want to be in this shop or around these items any longer. I am a true sport so I stepped back in the dressing room and waited for Ellie to try on a little, slinky, black, lacy negligee with thong panties to match. She strutted her stuff in the lengthy hallway of the dressing room, as it seemed other women were doing and I quickly admired how damn good she looked in it. Wow, those zumba classes she had been attending sure were paying off. Her muscles were on their way to becoming well defined and she seemed to fill out this little number in all the right places. I had to be proud of my best friend because she had worked so hard to get the body she was showing me. She had told me that the only positive thing about Jason leaving was that it had motivated her to focus more on herself.

"What do you think?"

"Gorgeous!" I said.

She knew I meant it because she has learned to read my thoughts and expressions so well. I told her that is the one. She beamed. I was thrilled to slowly begin seeing her come back to life. Good for her! As Ellie was handing the cashier her money(sixty five dollars to be exact) I hoped and prayed in my head that the encouragement or acceptance that I was giving her with this new relationship wouldn't somehow backfire. I didn't want to give her false hope. Is that what I had been doing? Was Madison the smart one for stepping back or was she just jealous because Ellie now had someone and she didn't? I just wanted to keep positive for her sake.

Somehow I had worked myself into stress mode and wished my thoughts wouldn't always get the best of me. I suggested we go to Sir Scoops a Lot for an ice cream cone. This place served the most delicious ice cream I have ever put in my mouth. Ellie looked at me and told me, in a joking way, that I must not want her to fit into her new purchase. I laughed and said, "One scoop won't kill ya!" My mouth drooled as I thought about the cookies and cream that I was about to order. My conscience was kicking me because it knew I didn't need any more fattening foods. I fought with my conscience (as I do from time to time) and won. Besides, I'm not a single girl trying to watch my weight. I had a husband who didn't care how much weight I put on—he even told me that. Ellie had ordered the smallest scoop of Rocky Road Surprise and I ordered two scoops of the Cookies and Cream that was calling my name. Sitting next to Ellie forced me to notice that I had gotten a little bigger in the past month or so and for some reason it began bothering me. Ugh, it must be this damn conscience of mine. I asked Ellie if I looked ok and she said I looked great. Isn't that what friends do best? Lie, in the most convincing way.

As I munched away, I noticed Ellie sitting there staring at her melting ice cream. She then asked me why I encouraged her to get this fattening dessert. "Don't you know how hard I am trying to watch my figure?" She dreadfully said. Here we go, I thought. The blame is already beginning. I wasn't going to take the blame so I threw the ball back in her court and made the comment that she didn't seem too concerned last night when she was scarfing down her five layered lasagna. "That's different, I hadn't eaten all day and that was my breakfast, lunch and dinner!" I felt bad so I apologized and knew I needed to make this right even if I knew she was misplacing blame. I then said, "You know, Ellie, not all men are like Jason. There are men out there who will love you for the beautiful person that lives inside you." I was really becoming concerned with this new attitude of hers that she thinks she needs to look good enough to be on the cover of Maxim. She said she had gotten used to having to look good for Jason and when she began putting a little weight on that's when all the problems began. I disagreed and told her that having to look good for him, in the beginning of their relationship, was when the problems began. She sat quietly and began eating her now softend ice cream. I'm not sure if she was eating it because what I said made sense or if it was because the melted ice cream was making such a mess. Ellie looked at me and told me that I was such a great friend and she thanked me for the encouraging words. Confusion overtook me at this point.

We shopped some more, but unfortunately I didn't find anything worth buying on this outing. I was happy to just be out with my best friend. We talked about many different things and I brought up Madison. Ellie told me that she was going to call Madison later in the day and things would be fine. She assured me that she has decided that Michael is going to be a thrill for her now and nothing more. This made me feel so much better and I knew it would ease Madison too. We wanted to see her have fun and not get too serious too soon. Ellie made a point to tell me that she is going to have fun like she did in her high school and college days and her little black negligee would help her with that! Ok, TMI is what I told her. We agreed that it was in fact a great day.

Madison had spent the day with James and her parents out on their boat. Sunday was family day for them and Madison would have it no other way. It had been particularly a hard day for Madison after James made the comment that he wished his father could be with them and that if he were there with them the day would be perfect.

Madison gripped her stomach at that comment and didn't feel well the rest of the day. She had reached for her Blackberry soon after that sorrowful statement had been made and scrolled through her contacts to find Seth's name. Don't do it, don't do it she had told herself. Her tremendous strength kept her from clicking on his name and she threw her phone back into the bag she retrieved it from. Then she got up, walked over to James and held him. This is the only thing she knew to do.

When James and Madison had returned home, she noticed the answering machine was lit up. She wondered who had called. She didn't have a lot of friends and that's the way she liked it. She didn't think Ellie or Brooke had called either. She picked up the message and stood with sadness as she listened to it. Hey James, it's your daddy. I was calling to see how you've been doing buddy. Will you please call me back? Madison stood there at a crossroad. James was tidying up his bedroom because he had promised his mom he would as soon as they got home. She didn't think James had heard the message as it played. She could easily delete it and not say a word, but her heart was telling her to get James and tell him his daddy called.

She had always had a special place in her heart for the father of her only child and she began feeling her strength weaken. She then did what she shouldn't have done and picked up the phone and dialed Seth's number. After the third ring, Seth answered the phone in a sleepy, lethargic voice. He could not believe it was Madison on the other end.

"Hey Maddie, how have you been?" He asked. Just like that- no remorse at all. How can men do that? She thought.

"I've been ok," is all she could manage to say. Those stupid feelings were creeping up from somewhere that she didn't think even existed anymore as she listened to the rehearsed excuses as to why he hadn't called in a while. He told her he had been lonely and wanted to see his son. Did that include her too? This she wondered. Why else did he bother to tell her he had been lonely? She didn't want to fight with him, but she didn't want to believe his one millionth lie either. "James has been missing you very much," Madison said flatly. Seth knew this was the perfect time to tell her what he had been wanting to earlier that day. "Madison, I have a week vacation that I am planning on using in June and I was wondering if we could spend this time together as a family?" "Are you freaking kidding me?" This came rushing out of her angry lips before she could stop it. He explained that he had been soul searching for some time and it always came back to him wanting to be with her and James. Madison told him that she didn't consider him family anymore and that being together during a family vacation would only cause more confusion for James. As much as she despised him at this point of her life she had also entertained the thought of having her little family back together again. How and why could she even allow Seth to be able to do this? Sure he had screwed up many times before.

He was young when he found out that he would be a father, but is that really a good excuse for him to have walked out on them? And his weakness of being seduced by a school girl was yet another mistake he had made. She thought that as strong as she was he seemed to be equally weak.

"Seth, I need to take all this in before I let you talk to James." Seth surprisingly understood and didn't argue with her. Wow, maybe he was changing. She told him she would get back with him by the middle of the week and they could MAYBE talk more about it. As she hung up the phone she wondered if she should share any of this with her two best friends. Spending time with his son would be great, but spending time with her was something totally different!

Chapter 5

Ellie and Brooke's week was going by fairly slow. Their students were hanging on by a thread. With their spring break right around the corner everyone was anxious for school to be out. This was the point in a teacher's career that made her have second thoughts as to why he or she chose to become a teacher. Not only was it crunch time with the many tests that were given, in hopes their student's scores would show much growth, but it was the time when even the best students started to break out of their shells and become little monsters. Although Ellie and Brooke were on the same hallway they rarely ever saw one another. Their schedules were different and some days they hadn't seen each other at all. It was amazing to work in the same building on the same hall and to not know for sure who was at work and who wasn't.

When Wednesday came I opened up my email first thing that morning and noticed that David had sent me a message. How sweet that he thought to do that from time to time. As I began reading it I became disappointed. He wrote that he couldn't make it for dinner and that he was going to meet with some potential person that was interested in being his business partner. Odd, I thought because he hadn't shared with me lately that he was seeking a business partner. Maybe that was going to be a surprise. I knew I had to keep positive to help him keep his spirits up. I sent him the message that I loved him and would see him when he got home.

Later that day Ellie called me on her break. That was a nice surprise since our breaks usually consisted of working and not actually taking a break. "Hey Ellie! What's up?" I asked. She told me she was so thrilled because Michael was meeting her after school today. I was so excited for her. "Is he meeting you here?" I asked. "No," she replied. "We are meeting at the park," she exclaimed. Oh how romantic! Maybe he will have a picnic set out for her. Would she be one lucky lady if she was fortunate enough to be dating a hopeless romantic! "Good for you!" I giggled. Ellie was lost in her dream world, but that was ok because for a few more minutes she had time to daydream.

The weather that afternoon was perfect Ellie thought as she got out of her car. The excitement was bubbling in her and she had waited all day to see Michael. They had texted a few times here and there that week and chatted a bit online, but they were both very busy people and meeting when they could is how it had to be. Her excitement was at an all time high and she was thrilled to know that a very intriguing man was interested in spending his time with her. Jason never gave her the time of day. He was always doing his thing while she tended to their children and home. She liked this new avenue of happiness.

When she pulled up she saw him waiting for her on the park bench looking as handsome as ever. He had a bouquet of pink carnations in his hand excitedly ready to give them to her. As she made her way over to him his urge to touch her grew strong. They hugged and he handed her the flowers. She held them and bent her head down to smell them. Michael always enjoyed watching a woman receive a gift such as the flowers he was handing her. It melted his heart every time. He told himself that Ellie was the type of woman that deserved gifts. They talked for a short time and he then told her he was taking her to a special place for dinner. This Wednesday was like no other. Her Wednesday's normally consisted of going home after work, making dinner for her children and grading papers. This Wednesday was proving to be a very special one!

When I got home Danielle was starting dinner. I was so thankful for that. An afternoon conference had lengthened my day and all I wanted to do when I got home was put my feet up and relax. Danielle is our oldest. She was a sophomore in college with her dreams set on a degree in science. As she stirred the sauce of what was going to be our spaghetti dinner she told me that Ashlei (our middle daughter) wouldn't be home for dinner because her cheerleading practice would be a little longer today. It looked like it would only be Danielle, Noelle (our youngest) and me for dinner. David seemed busier than usual and he was meeting that person.

At 9:30 I began to wonder how David's evening had gone. My eyes became heavy and as I was drifting off to sleep I heard David enter the bedroom. I had wanted to hear all about how his day had been, but I was so tired. When he climbed into bed, I noticed that he smelled of fresh cologne. I put my arms around him and he gently kissed me. He said good night and made his way to the bathroom. From the sound of his voice and his body language I guessed his day must not have ended on a good note.

In Madison's world things were changing fast. Her work had slowed to the point that she had barely put in twenty hours this week and she decided to begin looking for something that could be a little more promising if possible. She had called Seth back and told him that she and James would take the vacation with him. They had decided to go to Florida for a week and take James to Disney World for the first time. Madison thought this would probably do James and her some good to get out of town. Madison had told Seth that there could be no strings attached. This meaning that she and Seth would not sleep together as they always had in the past. Her strength would definitely be put to the test she thought. Seth agreed and the vacation would begin the week after school let out for the summer break.

Ellie's life was changing fast too. She and Michael seemed to be spending more and more time together. She had not introduced him to Katie Lynn or Hunter yet and knew it was still too soon. They had spent most of their free time in deep conversation and getting to know one another. It was going on three weeks that they had begun their relationship and so far so good! She wondered if he would ask her back to his place one day soon. They had been a little intimate, but nothing more than kissing and petting one another in those special places. Ellie was the one who would stop things from going too far. She wanted to take it slow and she felt Michael did too, but being male she knew that was a very difficult thing to do.

Madison and Ellie had begun talking again and Madison was getting used to the idea that Ellie had met a seemingly great guy. I was happy for my two best friends because they were beginning to find a little bit of happiness. My world was changing too and I wasn't sure if that was a good thing or not. David seemed to be on edge quite a bit and I decided it was time to have a talk with him. Sure I have seen him stressed to the max before, but it always had motivated him to stay strong. Recently, his attitude was one of giving up. I never wanted to be the meddling wife, but I felt like I needed to be this time. Maybe he was having some kind of mid life crisis and didn't know how to handle it. When he comes home I will have a nice meal waiting for him and then maybe he will feel comfortable talking to me about his work related problems.

It was Saturday afternoon and I was making David his favorite meal. The girls wouldn't be home for dinner so I decided to make it a special evening which included a candlelight dinner with soft music playing in the background. I would make it romantic and he would feel completely at ease. As I began preparing this delicious meal I became more positive about how the evening would go. He would feel comfortable sharing his worries with me as he always had in the past. The delectable steak would melt in his mouth and please him to no end. I laughed as I thought about the quirky expression that would appear on his face. In fact, it would be the same look I had seen so many times before as we were making love. Give a man his favorite meal and a good roll in the hay and you'll have them for life I thought. It was funny how men and women were different, but somehow the same. My mood lightened as I chopped fresh vegetables into pieces. I was happy that I could always find myself using my creative thinking to improve my negative mindset.

My excitement was growing as it was getting closer to dinner time. David would be home shortly. As I waited for him, I began to think that Ellie may be right. It was high time that I started thinking about putting more thought into the way I dressed and looked for my husband. Had he been slowly losing his attraction toward me because I wasn't putting enough effort into myself? I hadn't wanted to believe that before, but something was telling me to at least consider the advice. As I looked through my closet I seriously considered putting on the sexiest dress I owned. Why not? This was going to be a date. I hadn't worn this little number in probably a year! Wow, I really haven't put much into looking my best, I thought.

When David came home I noticed that he looked a little happier than usual. Maybe business had been good today or maybe it was because he smelled his favorite foods cooking. Whatever it was, it made me feel good to know that he looked a little less stressed and happy to be home. The candles were lit, the soft music played from the living room and dinner was ready. "Brooke, what's the special occasion?" He asked. "No special occasion, I just wanted to do something nice." His curiosity was running wild. He didn't think he had deserved anything special because of the way he had been acting toward her for the past few weeks. He felt guilty that he had not been treating her better. He had so much on his mind lately and knew he had been neglecting Brooke. He told himself he would do better. He just seemed to be questioning so many things lately about his business that wasn't doing as well as he wanted, his goals, and even his marriage. He knew he could talk to Brooke about work, but marriage that's a whole different ballgame he told himself. He knew wives wanted their men to share their deepest thoughts, but somehow he knew that Brooke would have a very difficult time understanding his new way of thinking. For their marriage sake he would tell her how much he loved her and leave it at that. Brooke and his family had always been solid ground and he was no idiot. He wouldn't risk losing any of them.

On the other side of town Ellie had just finished eating her favorite cereal. Jason had the children for the weekend and she had been feeling a bit lonely. She told herself not to feel this way and suddenly began thinking about Michael. She hadn't heard from him today which she thought was very odd. They had begun contacting each other in some way almost every day. His emails had intensified and he had actually begun sending her sexy text messages. They hadn't even given in fully to their desires, but anyone who read the messages that had been sent back and forth lately would probably find it hard to believe that a sexual relationship hadn't even begun. Oh she wondered when that was going to happen. She had been thinking about that more and more. She wondered how it would be to make love to Michael. Knowing he was the romantic type allowed Ellie's thoughts to run wild. Oh how badly she missed talking to him today. Her loneliness had gotten the best of her so she picked up the phone and began dialing Michael's number. She just wanted to hear his voice. Hmmm…. She thought. No answer. Voice mailbox was full. If I can't talk to him I can send him a quick text she thought. Hey handsome! How about you come over to my place tonight? The kids are with their dad. Miss talking to you. Call me. Did she sound desperate? Of course she did, but she was becoming impatient waiting for him to respond so she knew this would get his attention. Besides, she thought, someone needed to make the first move in this relationship. Now she would wait.

Dinner was going well in the Anderson home and Brooke was feeling better about David and her. He had loosened up and this put her at ease. She didn't want to mess things up while they were enjoying their dinner so she decided after dinner she would ease into the conversation that he would want to avoid. David was so pleased that this wonderful woman had made his most favorite dinner of all time. A 10 oz. sirloin, oversized baked potato with the fixings, steamed veggies and best of all Brooke's homemade coconut cream pie that had always knocked his socks off. He was such a lucky man and felt pangs of guilt run through him. Brooke had been neglected lately and tonight he would make that up to her. She was a well deserving woman and she would know that by the end of the night.

After their scrumptious dinner, Brooke began talking to David about the concerns that had been weighing on her for some time. Every good marriage had to "check in" from time to time she had told herself. "So baby, how are things going at the shop?"She inquired. "Slowly, but picking up a little," he replied. David didn't like to get too detailed about business ups and downs so he figured the less he said the better. They began talking more openly and this put both Brooke and David at ease. "You have been so stressed lately and I wanted to know how I can help you through it. David, are we ok?" I needed to know this before I went insane with the unknown. "Yea, baby we are good," David said. I had told him our lovemaking had slowed down and I was becoming a bit worried. He apologized and told me that he had been struggling with life in general, but not to worry because he felt it was a phase and things would be back to normal soon. All the things a wife wants to hear, but struggles in believing. I decided not to rock the boat and devote the evening to my adorable, sexy husband. As David got up to scrape off our plates, I grabbed his hand and told him "NO! Leave the plates and dishes and let's indulge ourselves in some quality alone time." David smiled and followed me to our bedroom. This night was going to last a long time and I, Brooke Anderson would make damn sure of that! I wanted so badly for this night to be a night David would remember so I had remembered (again) what Ellie had said the time we were together in Beverly's Boutique. Oh, I knew I had a sexy little number somewhere in that lingerie chest of drawers that I had begun focusing on. Would I even have enough time to go slip it on? David seemed wildly caught up in the moment and I didn't want to stop, but decided to ask him if he would like for me to change into something a little more naughty. He told me that he would love for me to do that and wondered to himself why had his wife quit dressing in that way for him years ago.

While David was lost in his thoughts, I slowly began to undress as daring as I knew how to be and giggled to myself. It had been so long ago that I had acted this provocative. Wow, I enjoyed feeling this way and wondered why it had taken me this long to come to my senses. I noticed the way David was looking at me and liked it. No words were said as we relied on our bodies to do the talking. Mine was saying how bad I wanted him. After slipping into a lacy, pink, hot little number I made my way over to David. I began moving my body on him in my most seductress way. This was not my style at all. I had seemed to always rely on David to make the moves and I'm sure he was wondering what I was doing and why did I seem to be throwing myself on him. He began to move with me and it was pure joy. Our bodies did the same dance they had for so many years and the familiarity with the new unknown were now beyond words. I wanted his dirty fantasies to be played out with me (his wife of 20 years) so I began straddling him and performing an unforgettable lap dance. Then I began telling him to do things to me that he has never done before. David was intrigued and wondered where this was coming from. We moved in rhythm and things seemed so perfect. David had the self control he needed to make this night last and we enjoyed each other's bodies for quite some time. When our lovemaking had ended, I lovingly asked David if he enjoyed it. He laughed and said, "Baby you are the best!" Things would be better between the two of us. I just knew it. This awesome evening in bed had proven that.

As I lay there with wonderful warm thoughts I looked over and watched David as he slept. He had been so stressed and tired these past few weeks. Although it wasn't very late I decided that sleep for him was more important than cuddling. I was full of energy so calling Ellie or Madison was what I decided to do. Ellie didn't answer so I tried Madison next. Madison should be home unless she was out with her son. As I waited and hoped she'd pick up my call I thought about how much time had elapsed since I had seen or even talked to her. She had sent me a brief text earlier in the week telling me that Seth had asked her if she and James could go on vacation with him. I wondered what decision she had made concerning the vacation thing with Seth. I decided to not judge her if her decision was to spend the week with him. Who was I to judge anyway? I just didn't want to see her get hurt again. By the second ring, Madison answered with a joyful hello. We made small talk for a few minutes and then I asked her what she had decided about spending the week with Seth. Madison paused for a few seconds and said, "James and I are going to do it!" Again I told myself not to judge. I asked her if Seth was bringing his girlfriend with him. She didn't laugh. "I'm just kidding, Madison," I blurted out. This was my way of being nosy. I wanted to know if Seth was still seeing the tramp he had started seeing soon after he decided to leave Madison and James. "No, Brooke. There is no one in his life and he told me he was lonely," she sadly said. Why would she even feel sorry for that dirt bag? I quickly thought. I didn't want her getting angry with me for my opinion of him so I just kept listening and keeping my nasty comments to myself. Isn't that what good friends are supposed to do? She told me the itinerary they had tentatively planned and most of it centered around James. I did think that was a positive thing that Madison and Seth were doing for their son. She stated that she and James would sleep together and Seth would have a bed to himself. I wondered if she would cave in eventually on that plan. She must have read my mind because she said there would be no hanky panky this time. I did not believe that for a second. Seth had been her first and for all I knew there had been no one after him and any time they had spent together they had always gotten together.

I asked Madison if Ellie knew about this. "Oh heck no," she said. She made me promise that I wouldn't say anything and I knew why. She didn't want Ellie to judge her as she had judged Ellie at the restaurant. The subject changed and Madison had begun telling me about how slow her work had become at the research company and she was going to begin looking for a new job soon. She had been checking online adds and noticed a position had opened for a CSI investigator. She knew it was a long shot with so many qualified people out there looking for this kind of work. She told me it would be a dream come true. The only setback was that the job would be 45 minutes from her home and she wasn't sure she wanted to travel. I encouraged her to do it and told her if she got the job everything else would fall in place. She thanked me for that advice and told me she was going to update her resume and send it via email. I told her how happy I was and I was glad things were beginning to look up. We talked most of the evening and it was good to catch up with her. I told her I couldn't wait to see her and Ellie again at Angelina's and that our gathering would be here before we knew it. She thanked me for calling and then we wished each other a good night.

Ellie had spent a depressing evening at home alone. She was having a hard time falling asleep and couldn't understand why Michael hadn't even replied to any of her text messages or those she sent through the chat room. Where the hell was he? Did he have to go out of town unexpectedly? He hadn't mentioned to her anytime lately that he would be going anywhere. Maybe he had to work longer today than usual, but that didn't make sense either. She crept out of bed and noticed the clock on her nightstand read 11:45. Fifteen minutes til midnight. Maybe he would be online. She opened her laptop and waited for her home screen to appear. This damn laptop was getting slower and slower she thought as she impatiently waited. There, she thought. She got into the chat room she had come very familiar with over the past couple of months and was excited to see that Michael had indeed left her a message. She clicked on it and read the following words: Ellie, I am so very sorry that I haven't gotten in touch with you today. I have been super busy and must have caught a virus because I am not feeling well this evening. I miss your beautiful face and wish I could see you. I will call you when I get to feeling better, Ellie read the message over and over and seemed to be over analyzing it. She had learned not to trust men, especially after what Jason had done to her. Was this a convinced lie that he was trying to feed her? Probably, but why? Hadn't things been going well between them? Hadn't they taken it slow so no one would get hurt? What did she do wrong and why was Michael beginning to pull away? She told herself to stop and take the words for what they said. Brooke had told her that there were good men out there and that she needed to begin believing that. As she closed her laptop, she crawled into her comfy bed, pulled the covers to her chin and told herself that Michael wasn't Jason and decided to believe that he was telling the truth.

Chapter 6

David awoke the next morning, feeling very well rested and clear headed. He hadn't felt like that in such a long time. He slowly crawled out of bed, not wanting to wake Brooke and decided to begin his new day. He planned to go to his shop and tinker around a bit. He typically didn't open on Sunday, but thought maybe if he did it would bring him a little more business. He would make up the lost Sunday church attendance by going that evening. David had made a pact with God that he would start going to church on a more regular basis and prayed that in return God would begin blessing him with more customers. He knew that he shouldn't be making these compromises, but he was desperate. He thought for sure that other people had bargained with God just as he had been doing for the past few months.

David had recently been having mixed feelings about his wife. He didn't know why because his wife was such a wonderful woman and any man would be proud to have her by their side. His interest had been waning lately and he knew his wife was beginning to worry. Why else would she have put on such a show for him the night before? That wasn't Brooke's style. Not that he was complaining because the attention was definitely on him and he enjoyed it. He began shoving his emotions far back in his mind, as he did often, and began preparing the opening of his store.

The day had begun and David was ecstatic that the beautiful weather had brought several people to his place of business. The weather was warmer and spring was in full bloom and David knew that many people would need seeds, plants, shovels and other much needed things to begin transforming their yards into creative works of art. He had struggled off and on internally with what he would do if sales dropped tremendously and he was forced to sell his business. He knew that only time would tell.

Meanwhile across town Ellie once again checked to see if any emails had made their way to her computer. Her mood began to lighten when she noticed that a message had been sent to her. But wait......it wasn't Michael who sent the message. As she pointed the cursor to open the message she asked herself who could be sending her a message from the chat room. Her friends didn't send her messages there and she wasn't seeing any other man. To her surprise she read the words in bold print: **LEAVE HIM ALONE! HE'S NOT YOURS TO HAVE.** Whoa! What did this message mean and why was it sent to her? Were they referring to Michael? Why? Ellie tried to figure out who had sent the message, but whoever had sent it did it anonymously. She thought to herself that this message sounded like a threat. Surely, this person sent this message to the wrong person. As Ellie sat there not knowing what to think, she decided to contact Michael. Maybe he would know what was going on and if he didn't she wasn't going to worry about it. Michael was a single man who wasn't attached so it couldn't be another woman, could it?

"Hello," answered Michael.

"Michael, are you feeling better?" Ellie had asked.

"Um, yea, somewhat," he replied.

She felt a little distance coming from his end of the line, but ignored it. Right now she had to get to the bottom of this little mystery that seemed to be staring at her from her laptop. God, please let Michael know what is going on, she thought to herself.

"Michael, honey I have something to tell you," Ellie said. "What is it, Ellie?"He muffled. He could feel a bit of urgency coming from the tone of her voice so with concern he asked her what was wrong. Ellie had explained that she had been checking her messages on her laptop and noticed a strange one just a few minutes before she called him. She read it to him and told him the letters had been put in bold print. He was just as baffled as she was. "Michael, please tell me you are not involved with another woman," she sternly said. He had denied any such thing and told her that it had to be a joke or that it had been mistakenly sent to the wrong person. She wanted to know how it could have been a mistake. It had been sent to her. That, he didn't know how to explain, but reassured her that it would be ok. Ellie wanted him to hold her right now and knew this was a perfect opportunity for the two of them to be together. She got up enough courage and asked in her sweetest voice if he could please come to her house and be with her. She really was a bit shaken up by this but not really afraid. Michael got directions to her house and told her he would be there within an hour. This isn't the way she had planned on inviting Michael to her house, but it just happened that way. This was a good enough reason for Michael to come over and Ellie couldn't help but to feel a little excitement in knowing that she was finally able to see him.

Thirty minutes later, Brooke called Ellie. Ellie really didn't have time to explain what she had experienced an hour before and knew she had to get ready for Michael. Ellie hated ignoring Brooke's calls but it had seemed lately that Brooke always seemed to call at the most inopportune time. Ellie didn't want Brooke to worry about her again because she didn't answer her phone so she decided to send her a quick text telling Brooke that she was super busy and would call her back later that day. Brooke didn't need to know every detail about her best friend's life thought Ellie.

Michael got in his truck and headed to Ellie's house. He kept thinking about the message Ellie had received. Although he had told her not to worry about it and dismissed it as something that was meant for someone else, it somewhat bothered him. Whoever sent it had really upset her and Michael didn't want her to be upset. Had this message actually been referring to him? His curiosity was getting the best of him. As he pulled into Ellie's driveway, he admired the beautiful home she and her kids lived in. He couldn't help but notice right away that the yard had been finely landscaped and he had wondered who tended to it. Michael rang the doorbell and waited for Ellie to answer the door. When she opened it he could feel the tension that was within her. She embraced him and said that she felt like she was in some strange way being threatened. He assured her that it was not a threat and then asked her if he could see the message. She grabbed her laptop and clicked on the message. Michael stared at it for a few minutes and was silent. He was trying to crack a code, Ellie had thought to herself. Whoever sent it did not want Ellie to know who they were. Michael still believed that it was sent by accident and closed the top part of her computer. "Michael, is there anything that I should know?" Ellie nervously asked. "Sweetie, you know everything there is to know about me and I want you to put this out of your mind," he replied. She smiled and told him she was overreacting and was going to delete the message. He opened the top part of the laptop and deleted it for her.

"There, it's all gone," he quickly said. He told her it was all just a mistake. Ellie didn't want Michael to leave although he had seemed to solve the problem so she enticed him to stay a little longer by offering him some lunch. Not a bad idea he thought. He hadn't eaten anything for breakfast and he was getting a little hungry.

"How does a barbeque sandwich with coleslaw sound?" She asked. "It sounds scrumptious," he said. As Michael sat at her kitchen table he admired the way she moved through the kitchen. Most women her age began putting on a little weight, but she didn't seem to have that problem. She was a little curvy, but that is an important part of being a woman he thought. Her curves seemed to excite him every time he was around her. Somewhere within his body he kept hearing a voice. This voice was telling him to show her how much he was interested in her right now at this very moment. His thoughts consumed him and as he sat at her kitchen table all he could think was how nice it would be to make love to this beautiful woman on this very table. "Here ya go," said Ellie. The hickory smell, coming from the barbeque, took him from his trance. He thought to himself that this woman not only could turn him on, but that she could cook too. His mouth watered at the sight of the sandwich she had placed in front of him and he couldn't wait to take the first bite. Before he could pick the sandwich up, Ellie had made her way into his lap and was feeding him the first bite. As he took the first bite, Michael told himself to stay calm.

Ellie knew she was taking advantage of the situation, but had waited almost a month for things to progress. She felt it was time to go forward with their relationship. After Michael swallowed the first bite she gave him, he leaned in and gave Ellie a very passionate kiss. He had tried to take things slow, but Ellie wasn't helping. She was so enticing, like that barbeque sandwich she had just fed him. In between bites, Michael and Ellie touched and kissed one another. When he finished the wonderful sandwich she had made for him, he gently stood up, leaned over and picked her up. Ellie was impressed. No one she had ever been with was as romantic as Michael, not even Jason. He carried her to the couch and laid her down. Ellie knew what was about to take place and she wanted to scream with excitement, but she kept it in and embraced the moment in silence. His kisses were so gentle and sweet as he ran his soft lips across her neck and face. This man was going to be a great lover she had told herself. As he began to move on top of her, his phone began to ring. "Ignore it, ignore it," Ellie said. Michael didn't even seem to hear the phone ringing. Thank God, Ellie thought. Clothing began flying in every direction. She could not wait for him to enter her. This she had wanted from the very beginning. The moment was so good and so right.

Their first time was perfect and this confirmed Ellie's belief that he indeed was the one she hoped would stay in her life. As Michael held Ellie he knew what they had was hot. This new romance was intense enough for him and he was falling hard for her and knew when he went home she would be the only one he could think about. For right now he just wanted to be with her in the moment and leave it at that. He lay there in disbelief that some crazy guy had let this one go. This woman was not hard to please. He figured her ex had to be gay or just plain stupid to leave this sexy woman. Ellie had thoughts racing in her mind too. What was she going to tell Brooke and Madison? Michael was supposed to be a fling, a boy toy, that's it. How would she convince her two best friends of this when they always seemed to be able to know when she was disguising the truth? He got to her and now she didn't know what to do. This was all new to her.

Michael stayed with Ellie a little longer and then told her he had to go. They both knew her ex would be dropping the kids off soon and Michael didn't want to be there when Jason arrived. Michael never wanted to meet Jason because he was afraid of what he might say or do to him. Ellie had shared with him all the horrible things that Jason had said and done to her throughout their marriage. Michael would get very angry if his name was even mentioned. Two grown men fighting in her house is not what Ellie needed and he knew that. They kissed good bye and he promised to call her that evening. As he drove away, Ellie watched him leave and suddenly began drifting once again into her dream world.

Later that day Ellie had decided to call Brooke. The two could talk on the phone for hours and not miss a beat. "Hey girl!" I noticed that Ellie's voice was higher than normal and I wondered if she had been drinking. "Ellie, are you ok?" I asked. "I am just lovely," she said. I knew Ellie had something very interesting to share with me. "What's up?" Ellie broke into this crazy laugh for what seemed like five minutes and I told her to calm down.

"You are acting like a mad woman," I exclaimed.

"We did it, Ellie. We did it!" She screamed out.

"Who's we and what did they do?"

"Duh, Brooke!"

Duh was right. How could I have been so slow? My mind wasn't thinking clearly obviously.

"Wow!" I blurted out. I told her no one was getting off the phone until I had every last detail. Some women would be a little embarrassed in sharing their details, but not Ellie and me. We could handle it and trust each other not to share these details with anyone else. Michael sounded like someone out of a romance novel and I became a little jealous. Ellie was so lucky to have found this guy. He seemed too perfect to be true and I couldn't wait until the day I could meet him. It was getting late and we knew we had another work week to tackle. We said our good byes and I realized that we were all very fortunate at this time in our lives.

Chapter 7

Time seemed to have flown and I couldn't believe that this Saturday would be our next Girls Gathering. This is the term we began using. We would meet again at Angelina's and this time I had a feeling everything was going to be perfect. Madison would fill us in on the latest news she had about Seth and finding a job. Ellie would continue sharing her trysts with Michael and I would get to tell them that David's business was unpredictable and leave it at that. We all had some kind of news to share and that I was sure of, and this would make for a great evening.

It was Saturday, May 1st and three beautiful women were getting ready to meet at their favorite restaurant. As before, Ellie was busily preparing her children their favorite meal and trying to get ready. This time, as she walked up her stairs with more lightness in her step, she wasn't feeling as negative as she had felt the month before. When she looked into the bedroom that she once shared with Jason the remorse and sadness were slowly disappearing. Thoughts of Michael (and not Jason) swarmed in her head as she quickly made her way to the closet. She had a new attitude, a positive one, that wasn't about to leave her anytime soon.

She couldn't believe a month ago today she had been so down on herself about her failed marriage. Today, all she could think about was how happy Michael had made her and how much she adores her best friend Brooke and Madison. She had also managed to keep her weight down and admired how damn good she looked. Positive thinking was her new mantra and there was no turning back. Now if she could just quit dreaming and be on time for once!

This time Madison's parents were picking James up. They thought it would be nice if they could take their only grandson out on the town. Madison was so very fortunate to have these wonderful parents and James was blessed to have them in his life. Madison was excited to tell her two best friends the best news she had been keeping secret for some time now. She hoped the girls would be excited for her. Her parents didn't even know about it. Tonight she felt like leaving her long auburn hair down. Her friends had only seen her hair down one other time. She had been feeling more confident the past few weeks and she liked feeling this way. She knew that if you feel good about yourself others will feel the same way about you too.

Ellie was the first of the three to arrive at Angelina's. She was so proud of herself. This was probably the first time she had ever made it on time to meet her friends. And actually she had arrived five minutes earlier than the scheduled time. This evening, her friends wouldn't snicker behind her back and make comments about her being late again. She had been making changes in her life and she was hoping that her friends would notice. As she waited, she fiddled around on her phone and began texting Michael. She had a few spare minutes to do this. Hey hottie. Whatcha doing? He texted her back right away. Not much Ellie. What are you doing? After a few friendly exchanges, Michael asked her if they could meet again soon. Ellie excitedly wrote, Sure! When? Michael wrote tomorrow. Sounds good was her reply. After Ellie wrote the last two words, she noticed that I had been standing there watching her. Ellie, how in the world did you make it here on time? I said. We laughed and Ellie said she was turning a new leaf and changing all the negative things about herself. I was impressed. Madison seemed to be the one dragging this time. "Who were you texting" I asked her already knowing the answer. Ellie blushed and I grabbed her phone. "Brooke, what are you doing?" Ellie shouted. "Oh just having some fun," I explained. I know what I was doing was a bit childish, but when I told Ellie that I wanted to say hi to her new love she just laughed. " Brooke, you don't even know him," Ellie said. "I know," I said. I texted the words HI LOVERBOY! Then I pushed the send button. Not two minutes later, Michael responded with a smiley face. Of course he had thought Ellie sent that text to him. Ellie told him that it was her crazy friend having a little fun. His response was LOL!

"Hey you two," came those words from a near distance. It was Madison. Ellie teasingly asked Madison if she was trying to be "The New Ellie." Madison knew exactly what Ellie was hinting. Madison wouldn't reply to that so she just laughed. We had been seated in our favorite booth per request and we all seemed to be very excited to be together and so far so good. There didn't seem to be any underlying tension as before. "So what were you two doing when I showed up?" asked Madison. I suspected there could be a little jealousy coming from her, but wasn't too sure. I told her that I was being immature and was texting Ellie's lover boy. Now this conversation could have gone sour if Madison still didn't approve of Ellie's online dating, but Madison seemed fine with Ellie and this guy. Heck, it had already been a little over a month that Ellie and Michael had been seeing each other. Madison was actually impressed. They all had so much to talk about, but knew that ordering their favorite drink had to be the first thing they would do.

Jessica (our waitress) wasn't working today. We had hoped for someone as good, if not better. An older woman made her way over to our table with a big smile on her face. "Hey you three," she gleefully said. "What can I get ya'll to drink?" I was impressed with her outgoing personality. She had a deep southern drawl that led me to believe she was from a town that was further inland. We each took turns ordering our Belinis. One month had passed since we last tasted these luscious fruity drinks. Soon after the waitress had taken our drink orders, a familiar face came to our table. It was Tom, David's best friend. We chatted for a few minutes and then I introduced him to Ellie and Madison. He had told us that he and his wife, Vicki, were celebrating their 20th Anniversary. We congratulated him and he thanked us. Ellie seemed to be fixated on watching Tom leave our table and I couldn't understand why. He was a good looking man of forty two, but the look she was giving him didn't seem to be a look of lust but that of wonderment. I asked Ellie why she seemed to be looking at Tom as if she was solving a puzzle. She laughed and told me that he looked so familiar. Then Madison said, "Well everyone has a twin out there somewhere."

When our drinks were placed in front of us, our excitement grew. Yum, yum is all I could say before slurping this delicious drink through my pink straw. We all got quiet and took several sips before we began our conversation. I wondered who would stop slurping first and begin talking. Not a whole lot of happiness had I been experiencing in my life lately so maybe I needed to be the last one to talk. Madison and Ellie's lives seemed to be changing quickly. New job possibilities, new men, past men, etc.... It was becoming difficult to keep up with these two, but I was very happy for both of them because their lives seemed to be changing and changing for the good.

Madison quit sipping first. I told her since she stopped sipping first, she had to be the first one to begin telling us all the details of her life since the last time we had all been together at Angelina's. Ellie agreed by nodding her head, with the straw still attached to her lips. "Ok," Madison said. She was so excited to tell them her great news. She had waited almost a week to share it and was busting at the seams. "I got a job!" She squealed in delight. "OMG," Ellie said a little too loud. I said, "Where is this job and what will you be doing?" She told us the job was pretty far from where she lived (almost an hour away) and she wasn't real thrilled about that, but she would travel back and forth for the time being. "What about James?" I asked. "Grandma and grandpa will be helping me out with him and he will be fine," she stated. She had told us that there had been close to 100 people applying for that position from all over our state. Ellie and I were so proud of her. "So what will you be doing?" Ellie asked. "I will actually be a crime scene investigator," she explained. "Just like Law and Order?" I said. "Yep, just like Law and Order. We asked her when she would start the new job and she told us May 11th would be her first day. I was so happy that she was beginning a new career and one where she would have more stability. She deserved that. Madison went on to tell us that she would be spending one week with Seth and James in June for the Florida vacation and it would be the week that they would go to Disney. Her new job told her one week was fine to take since it was already a pre planned vacation. She said James was getting excited about the trip to Disney that they would take next month.

Ellie wanted to know how things were going with Seth and her. "Well, he has been calling James on a more regular basis." "What about you, Madison," I asked. "Is he calling to talk to you too?" I persisted. A smile made its way to her face and she said that they had been more civil to one another and he was actually becoming like an old familiar friend again. Ellie, not wanting to dampen the mood with any negative talk, kept her thoughts in her head. He just wants to get you in bed Madison, were the words shifting through her mind. Ellie smiled instead and told Madison she was very happy for her. I entertained the same thoughts that I knew were swirling around in Ellie's imaginative mind, but also told Madison that I thought it was great that Seth was beginning to turn a new leaf. Who knows, stranger things have happened. Maybe Madison, Seth and James will be a family again. Only God knew the answer to that.

I told Ellie it was now her turn to talk and she asked me why I didn't want to share next. "Because I'm an old married woman and there is not much to tell." I really just wanted some good old fashioned advice from my two best friends. Some things had been bothering me for some time and I had kept these things bottled up for too long. Tonight would be the perfect time for me to get these thoughts out in the open. But not yet because I was too interested in the new things Ellie would be revealing. After we ordered our favorite entrees, Ellie began talking. We knew her conversation would center around Michael, but that was fine. She was having fun and maybe falling in love. I asked her if he was just a fling still. Not wanting to let on how much she had fallen for him, she laughed and said, "You know it!" This time I couldn't tell if Ellie was serious or not. Madison wanted to know if Ellie and Michael had made it to fourth base. How funny, I thought to myself. That is a term that we would have used in Jr. High and High School. That's what I loved about Madison. She was so young and sometimes that was so obvious. Ellie said, "I'll just say the man knows how to please a woman!" Madison burst out with laughter and so did I. I began to feel a little jealous as Ellie shared the latest details of her most recent sexual adventure. She seemed to be doing it more than David and me, I thought to myself. Lately, he was just too full of excuses and it was beginning to really tick me off. What man makes the excuse that he doesn't feel well or he's got too much on his mind to make love to his wife? Ellie deserved better of me. I would fake that I was happy for her. It was time that I began thinking like an actress since that's what I was planning my next career move to be. In my most dramatic voice I said, "Ellie, you are one lucky girl and I am soooo happy for you." I over emphasized the so but in a very sweet way. Neither Ellie nor Madison would even get the faintest clue that I was beginning to ooze with that green monster known as jealousy that lives inside us all.

I was surprised that Madison seemed to be warming up to the fact that Ellie and her online guy were doing well. Madison and I had never met Michael but had agreed that if he was a murderer he probably would have already killed Ellie and if he was married, Ellie surely would have seen clues by now. Ellie continued to talk about how wonderful Michael was and from what she was telling us it was hard to find anything wrong with the guy. Then again I thought David was perfect too when we began dating. It's not until we were a few years into our marriage that I could begin seeing those not so perfect qualities that resided in him.

Ellie and Madison were very much engrossed in conversation and that was fine with me. I didn't have much in common with them, it seemed anymore, but I was still their best friend and wanted to be supportive. Ellie decided not to mention the strange message she had received a short time ago from that unknown person. She didn't want her friends to worry and she knew Madison would be the first one to say I told you so. Things were going great tonight so why would she mess that up? Besides, she hadn't received another one since that day so she decided that whoever sent it made a mistake and sent it to the wrong person. Michael was hers and there was no other. She was sure of that.

Our food had arrived and as we had done so many times in the past, we each took turns describing how wonderful our food tasted. We always tried to one up each other by seeing who could use the most adjectives to describe their meal. Ellie had thought that one up. Maybe being a teacher really was in her blood, I thought as I enjoyed each new bite of my Fettucini Alfredo. "So Brooke, you have been awfully quiet," Ellie said. "What's new in your world?" I kept chewing and put my finger up to motion that I would begin talking as soon as I finished chewing. At this point I wasn't sure if I even wanted to share my troubles with Ellie and Madison. Why should I be the one to ruin this great evening? After I took a gulp from my second Belini I began sharing with my two best friends the concerns that I have had for some time now.

I began telling them about how my life with David had not been so great. I didn't want them to worry about me, but I felt that maybe they could give me some much needed advice or just listen to me vent. I just couldn't understand how or why my perfect life, according to Madison and Ellie, had started changing. Ok, here goes I dreadfully thought to myself. "Things have been a little strange lately," I slowly began to say."How so?" Madison asked. "Things seem to be changing between David and me," I weakly said. Ellie and Madison both stopped chewing their food and just stared at me. When Ellie had swallowed her food she gave me a smile and said, "Maybe it's just stress, Brooke." Stress can make people moody." I told Ellie that I had thought the same thing, but David has gone through stress before and I had never seen him so negative. "He wants to bury himself in work and constantly makes excuses to avoid being intimate." Judging by the look on both my friends faces, I could tell that I was facing a serious situation. I assured my friends that they didn't need to lie to me to save my feelings so I told them to give me some good honest advice.

Ellie asked me if I had sat down with David and had a heart to heart talk. "Yes," I replied. I told them that he always had an excuse for why he was moody or why he was so tired. To tell the truth I was getting damn tired of all the excuses he had been giving me the past few weeks. Madison didn't want to ask the next question, but she knew if she didn't Ellie probably would. "Brooke, could he be seeing another woman?"She asked. "Unfortunately, I have already asked myself and David that same question. "Oh wow, Brooke how did David respond to that?" Ellie asked. "Not good, he actually got angry and walked out when I accused him of that." Madison told me it was high time that I started being more observant. "Begin checking his pockets, his phone numbers and text messages, emails, receipts and maybe even begin following him. I had never not trusted David and I felt so low thinking this is what I may have to start doing. But they had a point. "Look, Brooke, we know it's not what you want to do, but maybe it would help you find the answers that you so desperately need," Ellie said. I thanked them for being there for me and giving me the advice that makes the most sense even if I didn't like it.

Ellie's stomach began feeling queasy. She began feeling those old familiar feelings that she had felt when Jason had been messing around on her. She couldn't bring that up and she sure didn't want Brooke to know that now.

She didn't want Brooke to stress any more than she already had been. No one seemed to know what to say and they knew this bothered Brooke. "I did not intend on ruining our evening and I feel that I have." Madison and Ellie had both reassured me that I didn't ruin the evening.

Although I sat there feeling ashamed and guilty of running my husband through the mud, I decided to tell them something positive about him. "David seems to be bringing in more business," I managed to say through a weak smile. My friends just sat there eating and trying to look happy for me. Who were they kidding? They weren't real fond of David at this point and they knew their friend could feel that emotion. "Come on guys, be happy for us in that way," I said. Ellie looked as if she were going to break and decided to keep chewing her food very slowly. "That's awesome," Madison managed to say in somewhat of a shaky voice. I thought to myself that what Madison and Ellie had thought about David and me in the past had disappeared in an instant. I would be the one they felt sorry for and would worry about. How did that happen? Life really could change in the blink of an eye I thought as I tried to swallow my food.

David was relieved that Brooke had left for the evening. He was getting tired of all the questions she always had for him and the constant clinginess that she had been displaying for some time. A man didn't need a woman who was so dependent and whiny. Brooke had never been that way that he could remember and he didn't like the new woman she had become. He had taken up a new hobby that he knew Brooke would definitely not approve of. He had begun looking at beautiful scantily dressed women on the internet. These women were so alluring and they didn't talk back or argue with him. This was so enticing to him. His friend Tom had introduced him to this new world and he couldn't have thanked him enough. Brooke didn't have a clue and he wanted it to stay that way. He had secrets of his own and wouldn't allow guilt to take over. He had told himself that all people have secrets, even married people. He was sure Brooke had kept secrets from him and for all he knew she could be keeping a secret from him right now. This was his way to justify what he was doing. He checked the clock and knew that she would be coming home soon, but before he shut down the computer he had one more thing he had to do.

The three girls decided to stay a little longer than usual at Angelina's. They had already ordered another fruity drink and were beginning to feel the effects of the alcohol. The subject had changed and we were laughing about the good things that had happened to us in the past month. Ellie was sharing a story about one of her crazy days in the classroom and Madison had laughed so hard she told us she almost wet her pants. Now that was funny. Madison let us know that when Seth had called her the first time she wanted to jump through the phone and wring his neck. The words weren't that funny, but the way she said it was quite comical. I even shared a story about how Noelle was practicing for her permit and she almost took out a row of cars. At the time I didn't think that was too funny, but right now with two drinks in us we found it hilarious. I was so happy to see that our evening would turn out the way I had planned. Before we left, Ellie had made the comment that when we were old and gray we would be sitting, side by side, in our rocking chairs and still be able to make each other laugh. We all visualized that and laughed even harder.

We departed with hugs from Angelina's and told one another to drive carefully. As I left the parking lot my light spirit began fading and I knew that once I returned home I would face reality once again. David would probably be asleep when I got home. This was what he did often when he was home. It's almost as if he didn't want to face the world so he would leave it.

The girls were in their rooms playing on their laptops. As I walked into our bedroom I noticed David logging off the computer. Well, I thought, at least he isn't sleeping.

"Hey David," I said as cheerfully as I could. He gave me a sheepish smile and asked me if I had fun tonight. I told him I had a blast. I walked over to him and put my arms around him. I wanted him to shower me with affection as he had done so well in the past, but he just sat there staring at a blank computer screen. David didn't feel like being affectionate, but his inner voice told him to fake it so he didn't have to listen to Brooke begging and pleading with him to tell her what's wrong. Hell, he really didn't know at this point what was really wrong anyway. He stood up and gently held her. He knew she had been drinking and probably wanted to be taken advantage of right now. That was his duty he thought. As David placed his wife on the bed, he began touching her the way she had always liked to be touched. To his surprise, she had begun to drift off to sleep. In a wicked way, he smiled and took delight in knowing that tonight he didn't have to please her.

Ellie was so tired that she hoped she would not fall asleep at the wheel. The alcohol had settled some time ago so her buzz was no longer affecting her. She had been thinking about Brooke's issues and couldn't believe that Brooke didn't seem to have the picture perfect life so much anymore and it seemed to have amazed her. Ellie had never met David and at this point didn't have the desire to. She and Brooke had only met two years ago and the few times Ellie had been to Brooke's house David had been at work. Her mind shifted gears and she began to think about Michael. Ellie wondered what he was doing so she decided to call him. It was 10:15 and she wanted to hear his voice.

Michael picked the phone up after the first ring. After he said hello, Ellie in her hottest voice said, "Hey baby, what are you doing right now?" His response was: "Thinking about making love to you." Her body quivered when she heard those words and she thought to herself that there was something about this man that made her want him like a drug. She was becoming an addict to his love and she wasn't sure if that was a good thing. She gave him her sexy laugh and told him that it could be arranged. This is what he liked about her. She was a woman who knew how to be dirty, but in a classy way. She knew what to say, when to say it and how to say it. He couldn't sleep and wanted so badly to meet her. He wouldn't have to stay with her all night, just a little while if she agreed.

"Ellie, how about you and I meet at the park?" He was the adventurous type and Ellie thought why not? "Sounds good to me," she said. She had a blanket in the trunk of her car and knew it could be put to good use. She told him it would take her ten minutes to get there and he said he would see her then.

As Ellie pulled into the vacant lot her excitement began to mount. She didn't really like sitting in the dark in this somewhat remote area but she knew it would be worth it. She was glad she didn't wait long though. Michael drove up about five minutes after her. They both got out of their vehicles and embraced one another. Michael found it enticing that they were alone together outside at the park. He had always enjoyed getting it on in different places and Ellie was just the woman he wanted to be doing right here at this very moment.

They made their way to a bench and sat down. This was nice, Ellie thought. It was quiet, but they could hear the sounds of an owl in the near distance. Michael and Ellie had sat there for a while talking and laughing and just being in the moment. Ellie began snuggling in Michael's arms and this pleased him greatly. She needed him but didn't suffocate him. It was nice. Michael began touching her breasts and no words were exchanged. They kissed and enjoyed one another. She needed him and he needed her. Ellie whispered that she had a blanket in the trunk of her car that they could lie on. Michael seemed pleased that Ellie was taking charge. He took her hand and they walked together to her car. Michael placed the blanket over Ellie's shoulders as they began walking back to where they had been. Ellie mo-tioned for Michael to follow her to a flat grassy area where she thought would be the perfect place to become one. Michael eagerly followed her to the spot where she had begun spreading her blanket and he watched her in the light of the moon.

Ellie giggled and Michael wanted to know what was so funny. She said their first time had been on her couch and now their second time would be on the grass. "When are we going to make love in a bed like most people do?" She giggled. He smiled and told her as long as he could be with her it didn't matter to him. She thought that to be such a sweet comment. He had wanted her since the last time they had been together, but he didn't want her to see him as a desperate man. They rolled around a bit in a playful manner, almost as a mating ritual, and then began to get a little more serious. It wasn't long that Ellie was removing Michael's clothes. They lay there naked and it felt so natural. The night air was a little cooler than usual and this made it perfect for him to show her how he could keep her warm. Michael allowed himself to explore Ellie in the way he wanted and Ellie seemed pleased. He knew how to time foreplay and had it down to a science. This, he thought, was one good thing that came with age. She wanted the night to last forever, but knew it couldn't. He took his time with Ellie and held her so lovingly for the longest time. She wanted to tell him she loved him, but knew it was too soon. She wondered if he was beginning to fall in love with her. By the way he held her she guessed it was a possibility.

They rested for a bit in each other's arms and it felt as time had stopped. Michael didn't have the intentions of falling for Ellie the way he had and began feeling a little scared. This was supposed to be a fun time fling, but his heart was feeling a little more than that. What would he do if she leaned over and told him she loved him? Was love what he had begun feeling? He didn't want to become stressed right now. What man did? He wanted to feel good, with no real strings attached, so he began touching Ellie again and enjoyed listening to her whisper sweet nothings in his ear.

I woke up in time for church the next morning and told David we would have a nice breakfast before church started. The girls were up and getting ready. I began making breakfast and told myself that this is just like old times. David didn't seem that enthusiastic about going and tried to make an excuse that he was too tired. "No baby, we are all going to church as a family and no one can make the excuse that they aren't going." David was so tired of Brooke acting like his mom, but he didn't want to make waves on Sunday. Not the Lord's Day. David slowly made his way back to the bedroom to get ready for church and felt an even more distance from Brooke. She had become such a nag to him. He had to snap out of this negative funk he was in and remind himself that Brooke was the love of his life and he owed her so much. Was this a mid life crisis thing like his dad had gone through? Was it hereditary or just a thing all men experienced? Maybe he could talk to Tom and get some helpful advice. But first he would get dressed, eat the wonderful meal his wife was preparing and go to church with his family. Today, he felt he needed to repent.

Ellie had awaken later in the morning. She and Michael hadn't left the park until 1 a.m. that morning. She slept wonderfully well and could thank Michael for that. She cleaned her house and didn't mind doing that. She was filled with happiness this morning and nothing could ruin that. She checked her computer because she thought maybe Michael had left her a message. As she clicked on her messages her heart began to sink. Another anonymous message had made its way to her computer. She didn't want to open the message, but knew she had to or her curiosity would get the best of her. This message said: **You are playing with fire and you're going to get burned!** Ellie's perfect day wasn't going to be so perfect after all.

Ellie knew in her heart that this message was intended for her and it made her very uneasy. Was Michael the fire that was going to burn her? Surely this was coming from someone who didn't approve of their relationship. Maybe a previous lover was not in favor of Michael and her being together. But how would that person have her email information? This mystery had her baffled. Perhaps Brooke or Madison were playing a joke on her. They did have her email information. That didn't make sense either. Ellie knew this would stay on her mind all day and this time she wasn't sure if she should tell Michael what she had discovered. Instead she would approach her two friends. If they weren't the ones who sent it maybe they could help her figure out who did.

Chapter 8

By Tuesday Ellie decided to text Brooke and Madison. She asked if they could all meet somewhere that evening to discuss something very important. These mysterious messages had been eating at her long enough and what she needed now was her friends help. Michael would just dismiss it as someone pulling a prank, but this she knew could not be the case.

Meeting at a little café close to where they all worked was the spot they had decided on meeting. Since it was close to dinner, they all decided that a cup of soup and half a sandwich would satisfy them. Ellie knew she could count on her two best friends for helpful advice.

"Ellie, is everything ok?" I asked. "I am wondering that too," said Madison. "Not really," Ellie said. Madison and I didn't think it had to do with Michael because she would have let us know about that sooner. She almost seemed afraid of what she was going to say next.

"I didn't want you all to worry about me so I have kind of kept some things to myself lately, but now I just don't think I should keep doing that," explained Ellie. She decided to go ahead and share with us her important news. "A few weeks ago I received an email that had been sent anonymously," she explained. "And?" I said. "And it said, Leave him alone, He's not yours to have. But that's not all.""Another anonymous message came to me a couple days ago." This one, she said sounded more threatening.

"What did it say?" Madison asked.

"You are playing with fire and you're going to get burned," Ellie quietly said.

Wow! I don't know how Madison felt, but I was beginning to get creepy feelings about this. "I need you all to help me figure out what these messages mean and who is sending them." Madison told Ellie that they could possibly be traced and that perhaps Ellie could contact her internet provider to look into it. I thought maybe she should block the person from sending her messages. Then we all tried to figure out what meaning was lurking behind them.

"I think someone may be jealous and they are trying to scare you," Madison said.

"I thought that too," Ellie said. "But who would want us to be apart?" "Does Michael have an ex girlfriend that may be trying to get him back," I asked.

"Possibly," she said.

"You better ask him about it," I warned.

The more Ellie thought about it, the more she began thinking that a scorned lover could be the culprit in these mystery messages. It's the only thing that made sense. A bored teenager, playing games on the internet just didn't seem likely anymore.

"Well it looks like your life has gotten very interesting lately, Ellie," Madison said. I agreed.

Ellie really didn't want Michael to have to dig up his past, but this was interfering with her life and she knew it had to be dealt with. If there was a possibility that an ex scorned lover was trying to intimidate her, they would wish they hadn't started something that she intended on finishing. She felt so much better knowing her friends were supporting her in this way. Their assurance meant so much to her. By the end of their conversation on this topic, they had all come to the agreement that it had to be an ex who had more time on her hands than needed. Ellie was confident that things would improve and felt more at ease.

Although my evening was going to be filled with working on report cards, I knew in my heart that meeting Ellie was the most important thing that I needed to do. Driving home, I began wondering what David and the girls were doing. When I got home I sat down at my computer to begin working on report cards, I noticed something interesting. A new file had been added to our computer that hadn't been there before. I clicked on it and wished I hadn't.

What the hell? These were my first thoughts as I stared at pictures of women, who I had never seen before, not wearing a whole lot of anything. David has hit rock bottom I began whispering to myself. Why would he be looking at these younger women, all whom appeared to be in their late 20's and early 30's. Was he intending on meeting any of them? Did he leave this file on the computer for me to find? Was this his guilty way of showing me why he had become so distant so fast? Questions were rapidly bouncing around in my head and I began feeling light headed. Our marriage really was going down the tubes and I didn't know what to do. He would have to face what he had been doing and I wasn't going to be nice this time and listen to the nonsense excuses he continually gave to me. If he was going to act like a child then I was going to treat him like one!

Madison had begun thinking about items she needed to pack for Disney. It would be here before she knew it and once she started work she knew she wouldn't have a whole lot of time to prepare. James had been so excited to know that he was going to be like his friends and get to go on a vacation with both his parents. That was a rare thing for James. He had been talking to his dad almost nightly and Madison began thinking that maybe the girl Seth had been dating was the one who was keeping him from his son. Rude bitch! She thought to her herself. Now that the tramp was out of his life, maybe, just maybe Madison could slide back into that available spot.

Ellie decided to not even check her messages on her computer because she wanted to avoid what may be there. Stop being silly, Ellie- just block this crazy person! She decided to open her laptop and see what she may find. Nothing, nothing was there. She felt relieved at that. Maybe next time she would actually write a message back to them. She had more important things to do than stand and wait at her computer for some loser to waste her time. Her children needed attention and once the evening had turned to night and her kids were tucked in she would wait for Michael to call.

By the look on Brooke's face, David knew he was in hot water. What in the world did he do this time? Brooke stood in the doorway with her hands on her hips and her lips stiff with anger. She looked like she was going to pounce on him at any minute and David knew that whatever he had done was the worst thing yet. "Brooke, what is the matter?" He cautiously asked. His wife pointed to the computer without saying a word. It didn't take David long to figure out that she had found his stash of collected pictures that he had saved in a file. He had meant to put that file in a place that she wouldn't find, but he had totally forgotten to do that. His memory was not what it had been even five years ago. He had stood there not knowing what to say. How could he have been that stupid? But then he began thinking that it was no different than having girlie magazines! Most of his friends had those and also stored pictures on their computers and their wives didn't seem to mind. Why was she so edgy about this anyway?

"David, who are those girls?"

He could lie and tell her they were random pictures of girls he didn't even know, but he wasn't sure how much information she already had and for all he knew she was merely testing him to see if he would tell the truth. She was good at doing that. His wife was too smart. Being married to a teacher was so difficult at times. Teachers always seem to know when someone is up to something.

David walked over to Brooke and put his arms around her and gave her that loving look that had always seemed to work. But this time he wasn't sure if his wife was going to soften. Her body was so tense and he didn't like the way she was refusing to respond to him.

I told him that I was so sick and tired of the lies and it was time that he helped me understand what was going on. David put his face in his hands and began to weep. The only other time I had seen my strong husband cry was when his father had passed a few years back. I didn't know whether to feel sorry for him or kick him while he was down. He had been so hard to get along with for the past couple months and the truth had become a stranger to him. I sat down next to my husband, my soul mate, and didn't say a word. I was at a loss for words and sat in silence. For better or for worse were the only words that resounded in my head.

David had gotten himself in too deep and he wasn't sure if his wife could help him. He was scared to share how he had been feeling and the other things he felt she needed to know. This was his wife, best friend and soul mate so why was it so hard for him to open his heart and pour it all out? A war was going on in his mind and he knew he had to start talking before he went insane.

"Brooke, I am so sorry that I have been an idiot lately and there is no excuse for my bad behavior. I really want to change." He sadly proclaimed.

"Are we going to be ok, or do we need to seek professional help?" I asked.

"Oh honey, let's try to work this out on our own and not drag a stranger into this," he said.

I told him that I wasn't sure if we could do this on our own because we have never been through problems to this extreme. "Maybe we just need to focus on each other a little more and spend a little more time together," he begged. I looked at the computer and told him to take the file, that I didn't approve of, and place it in the recycle bin and to not think about replacing that file with a new one. David slowly smiled and said, "I'm taking care of it right now."

David decided it was time he needed to take his wife on a date, something he hadn't done in a long time. Dinner and a movie were just what Brooke needed, he told himself. David knew that he had to overcome his weak feelings and remind himself that Brooke is the woman he chose to live the rest of his life with and fantasies would have to stay in his head and not out in the open where they could so easily be found! Maybe when things calmed down Brooke could become like those other wives, but then again David knew Brooke wasn't like most wives and would probably never accept fantasies that didn't involve her.

The next evening I was so excited when David asked me to dinner. I felt as if we had just started dating again. I told him that I was in the mood for Mexican so he told me to get ready and that's what we would have for dinner. As I was getting ready, I thought about our first date. Twenty three years ago a much younger David had finally gotten up the nerve to ask me if I wanted to go out sometime. I thought about how cute he was standing there, so awkwardly, waiting for my reply. When I told him yes, the biggest smile found its way on his face and I was hooked. That boyish smile and beautiful, crystal blue eyes are what reeled me in and I knew there was no turning back. The rest is history. Some years down the road he had confessed to me that the first time he ever saw me he knew I was the woman he would spend the rest of his life with. This is the David that I had fallen in love with and I am hoping with all I have that this David still lives somewhere within the familiar stranger I have come to know lately.

Hey baby! Been missing you. Call me when you can. Can't wait til you get back home. This is what Ellie had texted Michael earlier in the day and had been waiting so eagerly for a reply. She seemed to be acting somewhat desperate lately. Michael had told her he would be out of town for business and that he would possibly be coming back today. She hadn't heard from him yet and she figured that he must have been extremely busy to not have even texted her back.

Things had been great the past few weeks between Ellie and Michael and she didn't want to run him away. She knew if she began questioning him as to why he hadn't called her today, it may have damaging effects. She didn't want to be single again. She hated being single. Ellie had missed everything about Michael the past few days. She missed his smile, his gentle words, and even the way he smelled. The text she sent would hopefully put a smile on his face.

Chapter 9

Summer had officially begun. It was June 3rd and Madison had been running around crazily cleaning her house, packing last minute items and working a little extra due to her new job. This was her dream job and she couldn't have been happier. She was even going to miss her job while she was away, but she knew it would be waiting for her when she got back. How blessed she truly was to not only have a job, but to have the one she had always wanted.

She and James would be meeting Seth at the airport in one short hour. She had made sure to call her two best friends before she left and of course she had to call her parents too. Before she headed out of her house she looked back at the picture of James and her that had been taken a year before and decided that no matter what happened on this vacation she and James would still have each other. With a confident smile she yelled for James and told him it was time to leave.

James was so excited to jump in the car and take off. Madison didn't know what he was more excited about, going to Disney or seeing his father. She chose to believe that it was both. "Come on mom," James screamed impatiently. Madison would have scorned him for showing a slight bit of disrespect any other day, but she decided to let it slide today. It was a special day after all!

When Madison and James arrived at the airport Madison texted Seth to see if he had arrived yet. Their plane was due to leave in less than an hour and Madison wanted to make sure they were together before they boarded the plane. She thought it would be easier to walk in together than to be wandering around a busy airport with James asking her a thousand times where his dad could be.

Seth picked up after the second ring and sounded excited to hear Madison's voice. "We're here," she said. Madison told him where they had parked and Seth told her he would be there in a few minutes to help her with the luggage. James couldn't control his excitement much longer and was busting at the seams. "Where's dad?" He excitedly asked her. The poor boy hadn't seen his dad in about six months. No fault of her own Madison began to think. But she was a forgiving person and hoped that the disappearance of his dad for all those months was something that was not going to be repeated. James deserved a family and Madison was determined to win Seth back.

Their plane was scheduled to leave on time and this pleased Madison to no end. She had been dreadfully stuck in many airports in her life waiting for delayed flights. Today she didn't want to face that. She wanted this trip to be the best family vacation ever for her son. The flight was only two short hours before they arrived in sunny Florida. When they stepped off the plane James said, "Mickey Mouse here we come!"

Madison looked over at Seth and thanked him for inviting them and told her that James would never forget the time he was about to spend with both his parents. Seth put his arms around Madison and James and told them he was so happy that they were all together. Madison's heart began to skip a beat just as it had when she first met him. She didn't want to be a rebound so she knew she had to play this game very carefully. Her heart had been broken by this man one time before and she could not allow it to happen again.

The hotel Seth had booked was on the Disney property and was a five star resort. Madison couldn't believe how much timing Seth must have put into planning this trip. The hotel was beautiful. Palm trees surrounded it and a huge fountain was located in the front entrance of the hotel. It had two very large pools with a lazy river that ran from the inside pool to the outside pool. James even noticed a large slide located at the far end of the outside pool. A massage parlor was located inside and they had a full sized fitness room too. The place was enormous and Madison was very impressed. She wondered if Seth had brought what's her name here at some point during their fling.

"When can I go swimming?" James begged. "As soon as we check in and unpack then you can go if that's ok with your mom," Seth said. Madison was pleased to see that Seth wasn't trying to take over and make the decisions, but how could he? He hasn't been in James life so he really didn't have the right to do that or did he? "That's fine with me," Madison happily said.

The room was to die for. Madison had never been in a hotel room as appealing as this one. She had only seen this room in travel magazines. This room was quite larger than the regular hotel rooms she and James had ever stayed in before. There was a queen sized bed and a full bed that were decorated with beautiful brightly colored comforters and the beds were carved from bamboo. The room had a tropical theme. Madison had decided, as she looked around the room, that she was glad she had accepted Seth's invitation. This would be a vacation her son would never forget.

As Seth and Madison sat by the pool watching James bob up and down in the water, they talked about things that were taking place currently in each other's lives. Seth was very relieved that Madison didn't seem to be holding a grudge toward him for all the stupid things he had done to her and James in the past year. Madison had shared with him how she had started CSI work just a few weeks before and had spent the majority of that time in training. Seth was so happy for her and told her how proud he was of her. She had shared with him how well James had done in the second grade and that his test scores had placed him at the top of his class. Seth wasn't surprised because he knew James was one smart cookie.

They had decided to find a little pizza place for dinner. James had been talking about wanting pizza all day so Seth and Madison thought pizza for dinner is what it would be. The pizza place they chose was on the property and a large arcade was located to the left of the restaurant. James had never been in a pizza place with an arcade. He was beaming and told his dad he couldn't wait to play some video games. Madison was happy to be able to be there to witness the pure enjoyment that was bursting out of James. Which game would they play first was all James could think about.

Two hours later, Seth, Madison and James had arrived back at the hotel. James was worn out. The day had been long and good. James was actually ready to go to bed and Madison couldn't believe it. It had always been a challenge to get James to go to bed. They hadn't even visited the parks yet. As Madison sat there rubbing his head Seth made his way over to them. He knelt down so he was face to face with the son he had left so long ago. James smiled as his weak eyes began closing and Seth reached over and kissed him on his forehead and told James the three words that James had so longed to hear. Tears began forming in Madison's eyes and as she turned to look away, Seth put her face in his hands and gave her a gentle kiss. Madison didn't turn away.

When Madison knew that James was asleep, she got up and began to walk to the little patio that was outside of their room. Things were not making sense to her right now. This was not the world she had been living in and her better judgment was telling her to stop feeling with her heart as she had done before. She wanted to call Ellie or Brooke because they would give her good solid advice and listen to her, but she knew she had to do this on her own.

"Are you ok, Madison," Seth asked. "I don't know, Seth," she said. Things are complicated for me right now she had told him. They made their way out to the patio and stood at the railing looking out at the full moon that was glowing in the near distance. A sight that Madison wanted to keep in her memory forever. "Seth, what you did six months ago should be unforgiveable," Madison accusingly said. Seth knew it was coming and had been prepared for these words. He would take the blame for that statement because he deserved it indeed.

"I was young and dumb, Madison and I am trying to change my ways." Oh how Madison wanted to believe him. "Seth, what do you want from me?" Madison asked. "I want you and I want James and I want us to be a family again. I.... I.... would like for you to be my wife," Seth exclaimed. "WHAT?" Madison could not believe the words that had just come out of Seth's mouth. This was the biggest surprise she had experienced in a long time. What would Ellie and Brooke think about this? What would her parents think? Madison could not think at this moment and Seth just stood there seemingly waiting for a reply.

"So what do you think, Madison," Seth said. Madison opened her mouth but no words came out. She was in pure shock. Seth put his arm around her and waited for her to answer, but wasn't sure if that was going to happen.

Madison needed time, a lot of time, to wrap her head around the question that Seth had just asked her minutes before. Surely he didn't expect an answer right away. "Seth, I can't answer that now and I'm not even sure I will be able to answer that by the end of the week," said Madison in a confused voice. Them getting back together as a couple was one thing, but marriage! That was a whole other story. Seth understood and Madison could feel that Seth seemed to be on a whole new emotional level. She had only been with him for one day and she would have to spend more time with him to see if his emotions were really genuine. It had gotten late and Madison was exhausted. She told Seth she was tired and ready to go to bed. She decided to change in the bathroom because she didn't want to send Seth any mixed signals. After she slipped her cotton nightgown on and finished brushing her teeth she made her way to the other side of the queen size bed James had been sleeping in. Before she settled in for the night, she looked over at Seth, who was lying in the bed by himself and wished him a good night's rest. She turned the light off and knew that although she was extremely tired, going to sleep was going to be an impossible task.

Chapter 10

"I told you she was going to find out sooner or later," Tom said to David. "It's ok Tom. I have it under control," explained David. What David needed right now was a good friend, not a lecture. It seems that lecture was all he ever got anymore and he was growing tired of that.

Tom really was on his side, but reminded David how extremely careful you had to be when you wanted to take a walk on the wild side. Pictures and harmless chatting with strange women was one thing, but David had actually already crossed the line. David's game was the real deal and if he didn't watch it, he would surely lose it all.

David knew talking to Tom was the next best thing to being dragged into a shrink's office. He wasn't going to let a shrink determine the outcome of his twenty year marriage. Surely the advice they would give would somehow encourage Brooke to leave him. No way! He wasn't about to let that happen. But now his guilt was overriding him and he knew he had to talk openly about the things he had been doing for the past few months. He needed good sound advice and trusted Tom to be the one who could help him.

Tom had a sneaking suspicion that David had been playing hanky panky with someone else, but didn't know for sure. David was a quiet man who kept his thoughts to himself . David and Tom had chatted with girls from time to time on Tom's laptop, but it was all in good fun or so Tom thought. He had noticed that one particular girl had taken a real interest in David and Tom could tell it was getting a little too serious. "I have been seeing a woman on the side for a few months now," David proclaimed. "Oh man, it's not serious is it?" Tom asked. David looked at him and said, "Well it started out as a fling, but now I have strong feelings for her." Tom's face went pale. He hated the thought that Brooke, such a wonderful, beautiful woman would be torn to shreds if he left her for this woman. And what would his teenage daughters think? They would never forgive their father for this crime.

"David, end it and end it now!!!!" Tom demanded. "It's lust just pure lust. Your life will never be the same if you leave Brooke for this woman," Tom pleaded. David sat there not knowing what to say. He loved his wife with everything inside him and he knew what Tom was telling him was the God honest truth. "Tom, this woman has become my drug and without her I feel so empty inside," David said. "She is an addiction, so find something else that you can depend on that won't damage your marriage," Tom angrily said. "I'm going to end it with her. I have to. I just need to find something that will satisfy me in a non destructive way," David replied. He felt so much better getting all this out in the open and knew Tom would be the voice of reason in this situation.

As David made his way home, feeling more at ease, he thought of different things that could keep him from his lover. He would take up a hobby and maybe even Brooke could join him. They could go on a vacation and discover each other again. His business had been doing well lately and it was summer. He could find someone to man the shop and Brooke was home for the summer so why not? Now would be the perfect time to do that. Yes, there were different things he could do to avoid this woman who had crept into their marriage like a thief in the night. Everything would be fine, David told himself.

David and I are doing great, I told Ellie very enthusiastically. David wasn't home and talking to my best friend was therapeutic. Ellie and I had been wondering how Madison's vacation was going with Seth. We were betting each other whether or not Madison would sleep with Seth during this trip together. Ellie didn't think Madison would, but I told her it was a guarantee. We laughed and kept the conversation light. As I began to tell Ellie about my plans to get David out of town, my phone began to beep. Someone was calling on the other line. "Hold on Ellie, I have another call coming in." I switched over to the other call and said hello. No one seemed to be on the other end, but their number was still there on the screen. I said hello again, but this time they hung up.

Hmmmm....... Who would call just to listen to my voice?

"Ellie are you still there?"

"Yes. Who was that?"

"I have no idea. They just sat there and listened to me say hello. Wrong number I guess."

But this wasn't a wrong number. It was meant for her. Next time the caller would not stall and would tell Brooke what she needed to know.

"Brookie, I'm home," David said as he walked into the kitchen. I told Ellie I needed to get off the phone and spend some time with my man. Attention is what he needed and I was going to be the one who gave it to him. The pictures of those women that David had come to know too well were the last thing on my mind and I was pretty sure the same was true with David. Our lovemaking was more frequent and I know now that David was going through a phase. Men are like little boys who never grow up and continue going through different phases. That's all. "Hey baby," I said as I wrapped my arms around his neck. He was in a great mood and I could feel that the new David was slipping away and being replaced by the old (not so old) man that entered my life twenty three years ago. And it felt good!

On the other side of town Ellie had been keeping very busy with Hunter and Katie Lynn. Now that the kids were out of school she knew she would have to keep them busy or they would drive her stir crazy. Karate, swim lessons, and frequent trips to the beach were how she was spending her days. She knew being with her children would keep her from spending time with Michael, but he had understood. He was really busy too and seemed to be spending less time texting her. Their chats were few and far between, but Ellie still knew he liked her, maybe even loved her. She was going to get in touch with him soon because the children would be with their dad this weekend and she didn't want to be alone. She wanted to be snuggled in Michael's arms and feeling his love.

Hey Michael, it's me Ellie. I have missed talking to you and would like for you to call me back as soon as you can. This weekend I will be alone and would love to spend it with you. Talk to you soon. Ellie couldn't wait for Michael to call her back. She loved to hear his voice and decided that she would keep busy until he returned her call.

Michael saw the message, but wouldn't be able to call her back. He told himself he would call her later. He truly had been busy but also wanted to hear her voice. It had been a couple days since he had talked to her and almost a week since they had been together. A month ago this would have driven him insane, but now it didn't seem to bother him as much that their visits and conversations weren't occurring as often. The conflict of keeping a relationship alive with her and the possibility of him pulling away from her was a daily struggle for Michael. He was a gentleman so letting her down would be a difficult task.

As Ellie was cleaning up the dinner dishes, she heard her phone ring. She ran to her phone because she knew it had to be Michael calling her. When she looked at the number flashing on the screen she became a little disappointed. It wasn't him, but she answered it because it was Madison. She hadn't talked to her since she left for Florida and Ellie was so anxious to know what had been going on with Seth and her.

"Hello, Madison. How's it been going girl?"

"Oh Ellie! Do I have some news for you," she squealed.

"What, what is it?"

"Seth wants us to be a family again. He asked me to marry him!!!"

"What!" Ellie screamed.

"Yep!"

"What did you say to him?"

"Well I haven't give him an answer because I'm not sure."

Ellie asked her if Brooke knew yet and she said she hadn't been able to get in touch with her. Madison wanted to know Ellie's opinion, but Ellie really didn't know how to guide her. She only knew bad things about the guy so she probably wasn't the best one to give an honest opinion.

"What does your heart tell you?"

"My heart is saying yes, but my head is what needs convincing."

Ellie completely understood what she was saying. She advised her to write on a piece of paper the pros and cons of marrying him and hopefully the pros would outweigh the cons. Madison hadn't thought of that and knew calling Ellie was the right thing to do.

Madison went on to tell Ellie that she and James were having an amazing time in Florida and everything seemed so right. Ellie was happy for her. Madison had a great way of convincing Ellie that Seth was becoming a changed man. Maybe there was hope for them after all and maybe he was finally ready to settle down. Ellie had hoped with all her heart that Seth was being genuine and that the decision Madison made would not ruin James or her in the end.

Madison told Ellie not to breathe a word of any of this to anyone, not even Brooke because she wanted to be the one to share the news. If she decided to say yes, she wanted to be the one to tell her. Ellie agreed that she wouldn't say a word, but told her how hard it would be for her to keep something this big from Brooke. "I will try calling Brooke again this evening," Madison said. As they exchanged good byes, Ellie told Madison to take her time with this decision because it's one of the biggest decisions she will make in her lifetime. Madison thanked Ellie and told her she would keep in touch.

As Ellie finished cleaning the last pot, she let the water out of the sink. They had just finished a cheeseburger, baked beans and tater tot dinner and her kids were quietly playing in their rooms upstairs. She had a few minutes to relax before she would be breaking up a fight (she figured) so she decided to check her messages in the chat room. She hadn't had any anonymous messages lately and she was grateful for that.

When the screen appeared, that sinking feeling returned. There was one message waiting for her and she wanted to delete it but knew it would eat at her if she did. She had to see what was being sent to her this time. So as she clicked on the message she closed her eyes. One, two, three open your eyes, she was telling herself. When she did, she slowly read: **HE DOESN'T LOVE YOU AND HE WILL NEVER BE YOURS! IF YOU KNOW WHAT'S BEST YOU WILL END IT NOW!!!!**

That's it! She told herself. You my friend are being blocked. She did the necessary steps to block this person that wanted her relationship with Michael to end. Slowly, she began to breath and knew she would never have to deal with this again. Or so she thought.

Chapter 11

Madison's vacation was almost over and she was still struggling with the immense question Seth had shocked her with their first night in Florida. She watched James and Seth as they made their way to the next ride at Magic Kingdom. James wanted to ride every ride with his dad and hoped his mom would understand. Madison didn't mind because rides weren't really her cup of tea. She was fine sitting on a bench sipping a cool drink and eating a funnel cake anyway.

She hadn't seen James this excited in a very long time. It was pure pleasure to observe this and she and her son had truly had the most perfect week. Seth took them to dinner every night and the decision of where they ate was either up to Madison or James. This week was about them and for them Seth had told Madison when they exited the plane. Madison had to pinch herself to make sure she wasn't dreaming.

In five days Madison wanted to have her answer for Seth. James knew nothing about the question that had been proposed and Madison did not want him to know just yet. Seth had been a complete gentleman and not expected Madison to sleep with him. She admired him greatly for that. Who knows she thought, if he plays his cards right there may be a special treat in store for him.

It was getting late and James was growing tired so they decided it was time to leave. When they returned to their hotel room James had fallen asleep instantly. Madison and Seth helped him change into his pajamas and laughed because he was so incredibly pooped that he couldn't even sit up. "James needs a Disney World in our town," Madison joked. This place sure did have a way of magically putting their son to sleep.

Madison decided it was time to take a nice hot shower. The heat from the day didn't have her smelling too good and her hair was a sticky mess from the perspiration that had settled in it throughout the day. She told Seth she would be out in a little while and then they could sit together and talk before bed. This is what they had been doing nightly.

Seth had wild thoughts running through his head as he began to hear the water running from the shower Madison had started. What would she think if I snuck in and joined her? Would this be upsetting to her? Would he somehow lose the trust he was trying so hard to win back? Against his better judgment, Seth undressed and slowly made his way to the shower where steam was already forming on the mirror. Seth didn't want to blow the perfect week it had become, but he wanted her so bad and this was the area he found to be the most weak. It was a 50-50 shot and he was going to go for it.

As he opened the shower curtain carefully, he stood there naked watching her bathe herself. She had her eyes closed and looked happy and peaceful. He was so turned on at this very moment that it took everything for him not to jump in and attack her. He wanted to get her attention, but didn't want to scare her and that's what he was afraid he might do. He closed the curtain, stepped back and called her name from the door. "What do you need?" She joyfully said. "Um. Would you like some company in there?" He shyly asked. Before Madison could answer Seth was standing at the slightly opened shower curtain smiling at her. Madison felt so comfortable at this point and welcomed him into the steamy water that was cascading all over her body. Madison knew it was time to rediscover each other and find out if the love they once shared was still there.

Seth and Madison had both wanted to be together this week but had been denying it to themselves the whole time. Madison was enjoying the way Seth was feeling her body. He gently ran his hands through her long auburn hair and loved the way it felt against his skin. This beautiful, auburn hair is what he had noticed about her the first time they had met ten years before. Her smooth, wet skin was amazing too and he wanted this moment to last forever. Madison began running her hands all over Seth's body and enjoying the muscles that were tight under his skin. She loved his body and always had.

As Madison closed her eyes and let her hands guide the way, she became lost in her thoughts. She and Seth hadn't been together in this way in over a year and she couldn't believe they were together like this again. Her body was so relaxed and was screaming for his body to join hers this very moment. He wanted to be lost in the moment and enjoy her this way, but knew they both were too impatient for that. Seth began finding his way inside her and Madison shrieked with pure delight. As they made passionate love, Madison screamed, "Yes, yes, Seth I will marry you!" Once he heard this he became the happiest man alive and knew this time he would never do anything to lose her. Never!

Tonight, Madison joined Seth in the bed that he had been sleeping in the entire week by himself. Finally, he thought to himself, he would be able to hold her like he used to. Madison lay in his arms and told him how happy she had been this week but wanted reassurance that they were doing the right thing by getting married. He told her that the year they had been apart he really hadn't been happy and that the time he spent with his fling was not fulfilling. He was now ready to be a husband and Madison was ready to believe him. As strange as it all was, she wanted her friends and family to understand their situation and be happy for them. It would probably take time, but they would come around. As Madison began to fall asleep, she couldn't wait until the next day to tell James the wonderful news.

When David closed and locked the door of his store he thought that giving Brooke a bouquet of flowers would be a nice touch to the evening. He hadn't given her flowers in a long time and it would be nice to see the look on her face when he handed them to her. The florist by their house made the most unique arrangements. As he pulled into Gabby's Florist, he began feeling like a single man getting ready for his first date. It filled him with excitement and this he thought was a sure sign that things were going to begin turning around.

Gabby had gone to school with Brooke and David and when she saw David enter her shop she gave him a nice welcoming. "Hey David! How have you been?" She asked with a big smile on her face. "I've been doing great," David said. And he meant it. Besides she didn't have to know all the things that had been taking place between he and his wife these past few dreadful months.

"I've got some beautiful roses, chrysanthemums, and carnations that I can put together for you."

Gabby knew exactly what Brooke liked and David was thankful for that. David told her to go for it. As Gabby began placing the flowers together in an arrangement David walked around the small store and admired her talent. He had to admire the creativity that flowed from Gabby and seemed to find its way into her finished products. She was a talented woman. David made his way back to the counter where Gabby was carefully placing the red and pink roses, multicolored carnations and yellow mums in a way that each flower complimented the other. Sprigs of baby's breath were placed between the flowers adding a soft touch.

"Wow, Gabby you always seem to know what Brooke likes!"

"David I know what most women like," she laughed.

"I haven't seen Brooke in a while. What has she been up to?"

"She just started her summer break so actually she isn't up to a whole lot of anything," David chuckled.

Gabby looked at David as he stood there. She had always found him to be an attractive man and thought Brooke was one lucky lady. Gabby thought to herself that she wished someone like David would have married her. She was not that fortunate. The man she married several years back had become an alcoholic and taken her for what he could. He was a low life, no good, whiskey drinking snake and she curses the day she met him. Women like Brooke just didn't know how lucky they had it, but that didn't mean that

Gabby despised her. It just made her question why some women seem to have it made and often take it for granted.

"Why don't you tell Brooke to stop by sometime and she and I can catch up?" Gabby said happily. "I will," said David. David explained that one of Brooke's best friends was out of town and her other friend had been busy and this was leaving her a bit lonely.

"Well then she definitely has to come by one day."

"I'm sure she would like to and I will let her know that you would like to see her when I get home."

Gabby wasn't really lonely and really didn't rely on company because she kept herself busy making arrangements, filling orders and keeping busy with her newly created web page she had developed a few weeks ago. She was curious to find out what she could from Brooke about the current status of their marriage. It was a small town and rumor had already made its way to her little shop that Brooke and David's marriage was facing some troubled waters. She would comfort Brooke while Brooke spilled the beans. No, Gabby's life was not lonely just a little boring at times and a little drama is what she always looked forward to. Her next thoughts being maybe if they were facing divorce, David would be an eligible bachelor. A girl could only dream.

When the arrangement was complete, David told her how elegant it looked and Gabby seemed pleased with her work. David paid for the flowers, got in his truck and headed home. He couldn't wait to see the expression on Brooke's face when he handed her the flowers.

"Close your eyes," David said.

"Why?"

"Just do it," he pleaded.

"Alright."

"These are for you, my beautiful angel."

When I opened my eyes, I excitedly reached for the most spectacular flower arrangement I had ever seen. Before David would release them, he leaned in and planted the sweetest, warmest kiss on my lips. This kiss was a genuine kiss that had long been missed.

"I love you, David!"

"And I love you, Brooke Anderson!"

The whole family was together for dinner and I was ecstatic. It was very rare that our family ever came together to eat a meal. Teenagers were always on the go, I had told Ellie and Madison some time ago. But they had a hard time relating to that because their children were still so young. During dinner our daughters were busily chatting about all the different things they had planned to do that week that centered around their work schedules. Noelle was excited to land her first job at an ice cream shop and would be starting the following week. It seemed like old times. David, as usual, was not being able to get a word in inch wise, the girls giggling and sharing the latest news of what's been going on in their world, the only world that counted, and me listening and trying to follow each conversation. I had missed this time and I think David had too. When our girls were younger things just seemed to fall in place. It was a combined effort to raise our girls in a healthy, happy home and somehow that all changed over the past few years. Sure change was inevitable, but for some reason David and I didn't learn how to accept it.

Ashlei stopped chatting and admired the recently purchased flowers that I had placed in the center of the dining room table. "Where did those flowers come from?" She asked. I told her that her father brought them home. "They are gorgeous, mom," Danielle stated. "Yes they are and your father is a very special man," I said. David knew at this point that his wife and daughters were the most important people in the world and he would make it a conscious effort to show them that as often as he could.

When dinner was over, the girls told their parents to go relax because they were going to clean the dishes. That was a miracle. They must have figured that David and I needed to have some alone time. We thanked them and made our way out to the patio area that David had designed the summer before. The sky was beginning to set and we observed a most beautiful display of colors. Reds and pinks joined together as if an artist had used just the perfect colors to construct a new masterpiece. The newly planted flowers that David had planted a few weeks before were blooming wildly and signs of summer were all around us. What a perfect evening it truly was.

"Oh, I meant to tell you, Brooke. Gabby wants you to come by her shop sometime. She misses talking to you."

I laughed to myself because I knew why she wanted me to come by. She thrived on gossip and everyone knew that. Don't get me wrong, Gabby is a sweet girl, but that was one thing that she needed to change about herself.

"Oh really? David, you know the only reason she wants me to come by is to fill her in on our relationship." He was convinced that Gabby was genuine when she had said that. "David, she's a lonely woman and somehow learning about others misfortunes makes her feel better about herself. Trust me, I've know Gabby for a very long time and that is who she is. But I will go visit her soon."

"Do you think a lot of people know about our problems?" David asked. I told him I didn't know, but I wasn't going to worry about it. He laughed and wondered if, when he opened the newspaper, he would find a finely decorated article about their "troubled" marriage. Being in a small town made me wonder the same thing.

It was so wonderful that David and I seemed to be communicating and laughing more. I began remembering what my mother had always told me. Out of every bad situation comes something good. I had to train myself to begin thinking like that daily.

David began liking himself more now that he had deleted that file of pictures. How could he have been that dumb to think another woman could give him what he needed? His wife was the only one that could give him what he truly needed. She had it all, he thought. Brains, beauty, courage, personality, humor. What else could he ask for? Of course he knew that these women had probably wondered where he was and why he hadn't responded to them lately. There was one who had seemed to have really fallen for him, but she couldn't guarantee him real happiness and he was slowly realizing that. Now Brooke, she was the real deal and his heart was telling him that more and more each day. As long as he kept Brooke his main focus everything would be just fine.

Chapter 12

"Hey baby, what have you been doing lately?" Ellie asked Michael. She had been calling him just about all day and she finally reached him.

"I'm sorry Ellie, I have been so swamped with work," he explained.

It was the start of the weekend and Ellie was hoping Michael could stay with her that entire weekend. He hadn't done that in a while and she missed it. "So will you be able to hang out with me this weekend?" She begged.

Why did he even answer his phone? He thought to himself. He didn't know how to pull away from her. He was trying so hard to get his life on track, but didn't know how to let her go. She was a great woman who was a ray of sunshine in his life. He needed to see her and decided that if he did, this would have to be the last time. He would break it to her gently that things were complicated and as bad as he didn't want to end it, he needed to. He knew this would break her to no end and that's why he kept putting it off.

"Michael, are you still there?" Ellie was saying.

"Yes, I am. So what do you want to do this weekend," he slowly asked.

"I want to spend it with you, honey."

"Wow, the whole weekend?"

He told her that with work there would be no way he could break free for the whole weekend, but that he could meet her tomorrow night. She begged him to stay longer, but he resisted. Michael told her that he couldn't stay long because he had to wake up early because Saturday was his busiest day. Ellie was a little disappointed, but thought that seeing him for a little while was better than not seeing him at all. They hung up and Ellie had a hard time holding in her excitement. Michael on the other hand was feeling quite the opposite.

The next day Ellie decided to spend the day with Hunter and Katie Lynn before she took them to their father's house. A trip to the movie would be the perfect outing on such a stifling hot day. They had been begging their mom to take them to a movie all week. She would even splurge on popcorn and a drink this time.

"Katie, Hunter it's time to go," she yelled from the kitchen. "You all hurry up or we are going to be late for the movie," she continued. Her children ran to the door in anticipation. Ellie grabbed her keys and made her way out the door. Ellie couldn't help but notice that her babies weren't so much babies anymore and that it wouldn't be anytime that her children would be grown like Brooke's children. She shuddered at the thought of that and told herself she would hold on to moments like this as long as possible.

Ellie and her children munched away on popcorn and laughed throughout the animated movie. Ellie still enjoyed rated G movies and laughed at the idea that her personal life was anything but a G rating. That's why she was happy to have her children. They kept her pure most of the time.

The times she spent with her children were special, but Ellie would often think about how great it would be for her to have a man in her life that could enjoy her children too, a man like Michael. How awesome it would be for the four of them to go to the movies together like other families who were in the theater with them. She admired the way a husband, two rows in front of her, had his arm around his wife and was laughing with his little girl. Ellie's children deserved that, didn't they? Sure Katie Lynn and Hunter had a mom and a dad, but not a mom and dad who were together. But, Ellie knew if she played her cards right, her kids would have that again someday soon.

When the movie was over Ellie told her children that they had to get home and pack their bags. "We're going to daddy's, aren't we?" Katie Lynn announced. "Yes, Katie we are going to dad's tonight," Hunter said in a big boy voice. "Yippee!" Katie screamed. Ellie was happy that her children showed excitement when it was time to go to their father's house. He hadn't been much of a husband, but he was good father who enjoyed spending time with his children.

When Jason came to get the children he noticed how Ellie had been losing weight and was looking rather sexy. He told her she looked good and Ellie was ecstatic. Not because she had feelings for Jason (those were long gone), but because it's something she had made a conscious effort to do when they divorced and she was happy that he noticed this important change. Eat your heart out, Jason is what Ellie wanted to say, but said thank you instead. She would be mature about it.

"Good bye my little sweeties. I will pick ya'll up around 5:30 tomorrow evening."

They hugged and kissed her good bye and told her they loved her. The sting got her once again as she watched her babies happily walk to their father's car. She shut the door and began to cry. Why was it so hard to let them go when their father came for them? Her sadness had come from somewhere deep inside and as much as she wished for it to be gone, she wasn't sure if it truly ever would be.

Ellie knew she had to get it together. Michael would be coming over soon and he did not need to see her this way. Snap out of it, why don't you! Ellie was whispering this repeatedly to herself. The sudden ring of her cell phone snapped Ellie out of the trance she seemed to have fallen in and she finally answered it before it went to voicemail.

"Hello," Ellie quickly said.

"Hey, Ellie, what are you doing?" Michael asked.

She murmured a bit and told him she was feeling a little sad because her children just left to be with their dad and she started feeling lonely. She didn't want him to feel sorry for her. That wasn't her intention. "I'm sorry."

Um the reason I was calling was to tell you that I don't think I'm going to be able go come to your house tonight."

Ellie could not believe what she was hearing! She had looked forward to his visit for several days. What was the reason he was backing out? First Jason now Michael, Ellie frantically began thinking. "Why, why do you need to cancel?" Ellie desperately asked. Before he could answer Ellie began sniffling. She couldn't control the tears that were streaming down her face nor could she control the crackle of her voice.

"Oh please, don't cry Ellie. It's just real complicated and I think we need to take a break ." "I don't understand. What did I do to make you feel this way? Please make me understand what the problem is. I thought we were doing well," she begged.

At this point, Michael knew he shouldn't have cancelled their date. He was going to do the right thing and talk to her face to face. He had to. He owed her this much.

"I will still come over, but I do need to talk to you."

"Alright," Ellie quietly said. "When will you be coming?"

"I'm on my way."

Michael's thoughts ran wild in his head. He didn't want to end what he and Ellie had but in his heart it was time. Too many restraints were on him. Sure Ellie was going to hate him for this, but maybe she could find it in her heart to eventually forgive him. Forgiving people was something she was able to do easier than most women he had known.

Ellie was distraught, but whatever Michael had to tell her she was confident that she could change his mind. He was probably stressed or maybe it had to do with the messages that she had been receiving. It was probably an ex girlfriend trying to get back with him and Michael didn't know how to deal with it. Why wouldn't he have told her though? That she didn't know.

So many questions and hopefully all this could be worked out. Ellie wasn't going to accept that they needed to take a break. She was determined to never let him go.

Ellie looked like hell and she knew she wouldn't have time to change or do much to herself, but then again what did that matter. Michael obviously didn't want her anymore. She did decide to look in the mirror. Her hair looked good, but her makeup was smeared and her eyes were a bit puffy. She would quickly get a wash cloth and dampen it with warm water and then she would apply it to her eyes. This would take the swelling down. Once she touched up her make-up she would look as good as new.

Michael pulled into Ellie's driveway filled with much tension. The last thing he wanted to do was upset her especially when she was already upset. His timing was terrible, he thought. As he got out of his truck he wished himself luck because he was definitely going to need it.

Ellie had seen him pull up and she met him on her porch. He looked so good and all she wanted to do was jump in his arms and stay there all night. Surely he would understand. They had become so close and had been seeing each other for two months. Didn't that mean something to him?

Michael looked especially good this evening and when he met her on the porch, he leaned over and gave her a hug. This hug felt more like a hug you would receive from a relative, not a lover. She could feel the distance and it killed her. "Come on in Michael so we can talk," Ellie said. He followed her inside and immediately focused on the couch that they had first made love on. That was a special day, but now he decided it had really just been an act that was done in the heat of the moment. He felt strongly now that their relationship had been one built on lust and physical chemistry, not love.

Ellie asked Michael to sit down. She didn't feel it necessary to waste any time. "So Michael, what do you need to tell me?" Ellie asked. No matter how Michael was going to start this conversation he knew it wasn't going to be pleasant. Seeing how damn sexy she was he did want her again, but knew that if he made any moves it would just be sending her mixed messages. And she didn't deserve that after all she had been through.

"I don't know how to tell you this Ellie, but I haven't been totally honest with you these past two months."

"Michael, what are you saying? Why do I feel like what you are going to say next is going to shock the hell out of me and make me despise you?"

Michael just looked at her and shook his head uncontrollably. Ellie knew that whatever he was about to say wasn't good, not at all. But as bad as it would be she would try to understand because she had always been a reasonable person.

"I am not who you think I am," Michael blurted out.

"Huh? What do you mean?"

"I have a wife. I have a family. I am a horrible person!"

Ellie crazily laughed and said, "You are not serious and this is just an excuse to break it off with me! You are a liar and a jerk and I don't believe you at all!"

"Ellie calm down, calm down. I am telling you the truth and it is time you knew the truth. Ellie, I fell for you. I really did, but I should have never asked you out. I was weak and stupid and don't know what else to say."

Ellie just sat there staring in horrifying disbelief. She slipped into her dream world because that is where she felt comfort. As she sat there in pure shock, she didn't know what to even say once she came out of her comfort zone. Michael had quit talking and just sat there waiting for a reply. The silence was killing him, but he figured he deserved that. Ellie didn't know whether to attack him or just sit and have a break down. She told herself to stay calm. But that wasn't going to happen. Instead she began screaming hysterically. "How could you do this to me? How could you do this to your wife and family?" She had totally lost it at this point and there was no going back. Her head was spinning and she was close to having what she thought may be a breakdown.

"Ellie please let me explain."

"Please do because I can't wait to hear the ridiculous excuse you have for this huge mess you have created!" The words seethed from her tight lips.

Michael began explaining how it all began. "Ellie, when I began chatting with you online it was supposed to be just fun and games, but when I saw your picture I began to really fall for you. I have had some issues in my marriage for some time. I was wrong for pursuing you. I am so sorry for lying to you and dragging you into all this. I actually wanted to leave my wife for you, but knew in my heart that wasn't going to happen. So I knew it was time, past time, for me to finally be honest with you."

Unbelievable was all Ellie could think. She was actually speechless. She felt ridiculous screaming, she felt ridiculous not saying anything and she felt ridiculous just sitting there.

"Michael, I don't know what to say right now!"

"You are a liar and a cheat and you make me sick to my stomach. You picked a wonderful time to come clean. We have nothing else to say to each other and you need to leave. Now!"

It killed Michael that he had put this poor girl through such an awful ordeal. This was not who he really was, but he knew he had to disappoint one of them and it wasn't going to be his wife. "I am so sorry," he said. Please know that I didn't mean to hurt you intentionally. I was weak and I hate myself for it.

"Michael, I just have one question for you," Ellie said. "Does your wife know that you have been seeing me?"

Oh why did she ask that question? Michael thought to himself.

"No she doesn't know. I think she wonders though."

"Michael as mad as I am with you, I ought to find your wife's number in your phone and call her," Ellie shouted. But Ellie knew it wasn't her place to tell his wife.

"Please don't, Ellie." Michael pleaded.

Ellie showed him to the door and told him it was time for him to leave. She couldn't look at him anymore. What attraction she had for him was gone. She was too angry to even think about crying, but somehow she knew the tears would be coming before the end of the night. She scolded herself for allowing this man to play her as Jason had.

Michael just wanted to sit with Ellie and comfort her, but he was practical and knew it was time to leave. Did he do the right thing by coming clean with Ellie? Of course he did. He didn't know what else to say to this broken hearted woman so he turned toward the door and decided not to look back. He hated himself and would for a long time. He hoped Ellie wouldn't figure out who his wife was and tell her what he had been doing behind her back. He was so wrong and he almost thought that telling his wife may be what he would have to do to clear his guilty conscience. Time would tell.

Ellie sat in her quiet, lonely house and stared at the pictures of her children that were neatly arranged on her mantle. All the pictures that showed her with Jason had been removed once he left her. She told herself not to cry and she didn't. She sat lost in her thoughts extremely puzzled by the incident that had just taken place. How could she have been so naïve to fall for this man who she had thought all along was a perfect gentleman? No one is perfect she said to herself. Reasoning would keep her from having a meltdown so she continued talking to herself. What would she tell her friends? They would surely feel sorry for her like they had for the past year and a half. As her mind began bouncing from thought to thought she began doing what she told herself she wouldn't. Tears came spilling down uncontrollably as she sat there rocking herself.

Chapter 13

Madison and James were on their way back from Florida. James was the happiest Madison had seen him in such a long time. Madison and Seth had told James they were going to be a family again. They told him about the wedding that was planned for December. Seth had planned on putting in for a transfer and moving back in with Madison and James once the transfer was approved. Things were looking up for this family.

When the plane landed, James began to cry. "What's wrong, buddy?" Seth asked. "I don't want you to leave daddy," he pleaded. Seth put his arm around James and told him he would call him tonight and that as soon as he could move back in he would. Madison hated seeing James like this, but felt confident that it would all be better as soon as Seth came back and they became a family once again.

As they parted their separate ways, James waved to his father until he couldn't see him anymore. Madison believed that things were going to work this time. She had so much to do. She had a wedding to start planning once she returned home. She had to start thinking about the colors of her brides-maid dresses, where the wedding was going to take place, how many people they would invite, the reception and so much more! Knowing that her two best friends would help her plan this wedding, soon put her frazzled mind to ease.

Madison had realized, while she was driving home, that she had not told Brooke the exciting news. As soon as she got home and settled in she would have to call Brooke. It was only right. Ellie knew, but promised to keep it a secret. Once Madison shared it with Brooke they would all get together and begin planning the wedding. She looked in the rearview mirror and noticed that James had fallen asleep. She thought about how darling he would look in a little tuxedo. He would be the ring bearer or best man at her wedding. Life was good and things were finally turning around for Madison and her son. Her son's biggest wish was going to come true.

When the rain began hitting the front window of Madison's car, she began swearing. She hated driving in the rain, especially when it was dark and her child was with her. She knew she didn't have far to go so she drove slower than usual. Her defrost never seemed to work when she needed it to so she began fiddling with it to get it to work now before the rain started pounding down. "Damn defrost," she began saying loudly. Come on, I need you to work, she fussed. The rain began to beat down harder on her car and she just about had the defrost working when she noticed that her car was heading for the ditch. She screamed and stepped on the brake, but her car began to hydra plane. It began spinning out of control and Madison couldn't do anything to stop the car. Horror spread over her and she knew there was nothing she could do to protect her son who was sleeping like an angel in the backseat. She braced herself and screamed while her car skidded into the ditch. "Oh dear God, help us!"

Police cars, a fire truck and a couple ambulances surrounded Madison's car. Fortunately, her car had not flipped over, but it had landed on its side, the side that James occupied. Madison was pinned in and hurt all over. "James, James," she began whispering. Are you ok? She couldn't move so it was impossible for her to get up and look over the seat to see what condition James was in. She became frozen with fear because her son wasn't answering her. Why wasn't he answering her? A million thoughts consumed her mind and fear began to paralyze her. She tried to look out the window, but it was cracked and the rain was making it difficult to see anything at all. She could do nothing but wait for someone to come to her car and let her know what was happening.

A knock on her side window freed her from her thoughts. "Ma'am, can you hear me?" A man said. "Yes, I can hear you," Madison weakly said. He told her not to move and to relax because they were going to be getting her out soon. Why didn't they say they would be getting her son out too? Didn't they see him? She began calling James name again. She tried to stay calm, but was becoming hysterical. She prayed a short prayer and pleaded with God that her son be ok. He was just knocked unconscious that's all, Madison kept telling herself.

The rain wasn't letting up and she knew that would hinder the amount of time it would take getting James and her out of the car. She wondered how long they had been there and was trying to figure out what time it was when the car ran off the road. Her phone began ringing and she wanted so desperately to answer it, but knew she couldn't. Her parents were probably wondering where they were or it could have been Ellie or Brooke wanting to know all about her vacation.

"Mom, mom, where are you?" A small, frail voice was saying.

"James, are you ok honey?" Madison managed to ask.

"I'm stuck," he said.

"Where are you?"

"On the floor and I can't move," he wailed.

"Are you hurt anywhere?"

"Yes, my whole body hurts."

"They are going to get us out and we will be ok," Madison said.

"Thank you God that my child is still alive," Madison declared as boldly as she could.

The firemen began cutting on her car with the jaws of life for what seemed like hours and finally began working their way into the car. Madison told them her son was in the back, on the floor and she wanted them to get him first. One of the men made his way to the back and found James crumpled on the floor. He carefully began removing him. Madison became very fearful that something could be really wrong with her son. The second fireman began pulling Madison from the car. Madison had to see her son and demanded that she get to see him before they went to the hospital. When Madison was placed next to James she began to cry. His face was swollen and cut and he seemed to have fallen back to sleep. "Is he going to be ok?" she demanded. No one would answer her. Her body went numb and she began thinking that this was all just a bad dream. They weren't in a wreck and she would wake up soon. She had to still be in Florida because the week had been perfect and this just couldn't be possible. Madison had to close her eyes because she was much too weak. "When I wake up, everything will be back to normal," she told herself.

Madison's parents were soon contacted and they raced to the hospital at once. Her mother would call Brooke and Ellie once they arrived. Madison's father looked at her mother and told her everything would be ok. But her mother had the most dreadful feeling. The feeling of gloom hung over her and all she wanted to do was hold her daughter and grandson.

Ellie's phone began ringing and she thought about not even answering. Why? It was probably Michael apologizing for the hundredth time. But something told her to get it and so she did. She didn't recognize the number that was showing up on her phone. When she answered it, she knew something was terribly wrong. The voice on the other end was shaking and she could hardly make out what they were saying. Finally another voice came on the phone and it was a man's voice. A voice that sounded vaguely familiar.

"Ellie, this is Mr. McDowell-Madison's father and she and James have been in a car accident.

"Oh No! Are they going to be ok?" She frantically asked.

"We don't know yet, we just got here," he explained. Ellie wasted no time and told him she would be at the hospital in 20 minutes.

"Mr. McDowell, do you need me to call Brooke?"

"If you could, I would really appreciate it," he wearily said.

"I will."

Ellie had no time to think about her problems because what Madison and James were going through was monumental compared to Ellie's troubles.

The minute Ellie got off the phone she called Brooke. Ellie's hands were shaking. She had to think positively, but she was absolutely distraught by the news. She knew she wouldn't have time to even check herself in the mirror, but didn't think that mattered right now. Ellie grabbed her purse and keys and headed out the door. She tried several times to reach Brooke, but Brooke wasn't picking up. She decided to text her before she started the car. She definitely didn't need to be texting while she was driving in this storm.

Brooke, call me immediately! Madison and James were in a wreck and they are now at the hospital. This was the text that Ellie sent to Brooke. Ellie started her car, put it in reverse and headed to the hospital. She told herself to remain calm and prayed for them the whole way. Right before Ellie made a right turn into the hospital parking area she began to think about Seth. He was her fiancé and needed to be contacted. She didn't have a number to reach him and she wondered if Brooke did. She had no idea what shape Madison would be in, but thought that if Madison was coherent that she could give Ellie his number and he could be contacted. He did have a right to know.

Ellie quickly walked into the ER and found Madison's parents sitting on the edges of their chairs. Ellie felt so bad for Madison's parents because they looked so miserable. She made her way over to them and gave them a hug. "Have you heard anything yet?" Ellie inquired. Madison's father spoke at once. "Madison's right arm is broken from the impact, but other than that they think she will be fine," he said. "James on the other hand….." His voice became shaky and Madison's mom began to cry. "What?" I demanded. "Tell me he's going to be ok!" I said. "James is suffering from a concussion and some internal bleeding." Ellie sat down next to James grandma and reached for her hand. "He will be ok," Ellie had told her. "We just don't know," she sadly commented.

Ellie could feel her phone vibrating and reached for it. Brooke was calling. Ellie stood up and walked to the entrance of the ER to talk to Brooke. Ellie's head was pounding from everything that had occurred that evening. First Michael and now this. She knew she had to keep strong especially for Madison's parents. "Ellie, what the hell happened?" Ellie could hear the fear in Brooke's voice. "I'm not sure, Brooke. I just got to the hospital and don't know all the details. You just need to get here as quickly as possible," Ellie impatiently said. "I am, I am on my way!"

When the Dr. walked out to the waiting room, Ellie practically ran to him. She knew she would be the one that would have to comfort the McDowell's. Madison was fine, well except for the broken arm and cuts and bruises that covered her he had told them. But, the same was not true for James. He had suffered internal bleeding and they had to operate on him immediately. Ellie wanted to throw up. Her stomach hurt so badly and Madison's mother looked like she was going to pass out. "Doctor, are his chances good?" Ellie began. He gave them a hopeful look and told them that they had no choice but to operate and said that all operations have risks. Ellie knew that, but she just wanted to hear that he would be fine. Ellie and Madison's parents knew that all they could do was pray for James and stay positive.

I zipped into the parking lot. When I walked into the hospital a tragic feeling came over me. The desperate look on their faces told me that the news was not welcoming. I quickly said hello to Madison's parents and Ellie. Ellie pulled away from the McDowell's to share the drastic news with me. I wanted to cry, but Ellie said I had to be strong. She explained to me the situation with James and I was feeling anything but positive. Ellie told me that we needed to find out if Madison was able to get in touch with Seth. I knew they had spent the week together, but I wondered why he needed to be contacted.

"When can we see Madison?" I asked Ellie. Ellie told me that we needed to ask the receptionist that question. I made my way to her desk.

"Excuse me, when can we see Madison McDowell?" The rather unfriendly lady told me that someone would let us know shortly and to please have a seat. I wasn't very happy with that answer, but I wasn't there to stir up problems.

We sat down and noticed that Madison's parents were huddled in a different part of the room together. They needed their space right now so we left them alone. Ellie and I hadn't really been informed with exact details so we decided it was best to just be patient and information would be shared with us hopefully before the night's end.

Ellie wanted to take her mind off this terrible situation so she began sharing with me the uneventful happenings of the early evening. Ellie wanted to break down while she began explaining, but knew she couldn't do that, not now anyway. I sat listening in total disbelief. What a scumbag I told her. Aren't you glad you found this out now before you were engaged? No matter what I said to her, I knew she was hurt to no end.

"Ellie, do you think Michael's wife was sending you those messages?" I asked.

"No, he told me his wife didn't know.

"Wow, then who could have been sending them?"

"That I don't know, and may never know."

I didn't know what else to do so I leaned over and hugged her and told her I was there for her. She said she had no doubt that I would be there. We couldn't believe how a relationship had ended and a horrible car accident had taken place in the same evening.

"I'm more concerned for James right now," Ellie said.

A nurse made her way over to Madison's parents and Ellie and I made our way over to them. She was explaining that Madison was in tears and we needed to go back and see her. Duh, I thought. We should have been able to see her sooner than this! We remained calm and walked toward the room she had been admitted to. I felt so sorry for my other best friend. She lay in the hospital bed helpless and crying hysterically. Her parents made their way to the side of her bed and Ellie and I just stood to the side. I want my baby, I want my baby is what she kept moaning and Ellie and I stood there holding onto each other.

"Madison, can you give us Seth's number and one of us will call him for you," I said. She continued moaning and crying. Maybe when she calmed down, she would give us the number. Madison's parents needed to be alone with their daughter so Ellie and I decided to leave the room. We would return in a bit. As we began walking toward the waiting room, Ellie began telling me how wonderful Madison and James vacation was with Seth. She continued telling me that it went so well that Seth proposed to Madison and she accepted. I was in more shock!

"When was she going to tell me?" I asked.

"Well, she tried calling you, but didn't get in touch with you and she said she didn't want to leave the news on your voicemail," Ellie explained.

My emotions were mixed. What if he's jerking her chain? He has done that in the past. "I know, but she said he was a much different person and she believes he has grown up and is ready for a wife and child."

"Well it's about time!"

Ellie continued filling me in with the details of Madison and Seth's decision to get married and we agreed that once Madison and James were better, we had a wedding to start planning. I love the way Ellie can be so positive in the worst of situations. That's the kind of friend everyone needs by their side.

While we were engrossed in our conversation, I noticed Madison's father walking toward us. "Madison wants you girls to come in now," he said. We followed him back into her room and noticed this time that she wasn't moaning, but tears were still streaming down her face. "Hey sweetie," Ellie said at once. I made my way over next to Ellie and said hello too. Madison began rattling off a number, a number we assumed belonged to Seth. "Madison, is this Seth's phone number?" I asked. She nodded her head and began moaning again. Ellie began punching the numbers into her phone and hoped to God that Seth would answer. She did not want to leave this news on a voicemail.

"Hello, who is this?" Seth asked.

"Is this Seth Graham?"

"Yes, it is."

Before he could ask again who was calling him, Ellie cut him off and told him who she was and why she was calling. Seth became frantic. He knew it would take him at least an hour to get there. He wanted to know details, but Ellie still didn't know all the details and told him hopefully they would know more in a little while. The last thing Ellie told him was to drive carefully and then she hung up.

A weak voice asked if Seth was coming and Ellie walked back over to Madison's side of the bed and said he will be here in one hour. This seemed to comfort Madison. We sat with her for a while without saying anything. We had never seen Madison in this much pain. Holding hands we sat in a void of silence. Madison was our best friend and we were going to help her in whatever way she needed us to because that's what friends do for each other.

When Seth arrived an hour later, he ran to her room and embraced her. Although Madison's parents didn't think too kindly of Seth, they were happy to see that he was able to be there for her. He held her and told her everything was going to be fine. She listened to him and began believing this too. We introduced ourselves and told him that we were glad to meet him. He probably had his doubts about that, but didn't let on. He seemed very nice and showed much concern for his future wife and son. As we made light conversation, a nurse came in and told us the doctor wanted to talk to us. I knew someone had to stay with Madison. I told everyone that I would sit with her. I said a prayer in my head that James was going to be fine and had faith that God would answer my prayer- all of our prayers.

Madison had fallen asleep due to the medication they had given her. When Seth walked into the room I felt relieved. His body language and smile told me that James was going to be alright. Before I could ask, this stranger picked me up and hugged me. He excitedly shouted, "My son is going to be ok!" I hugged him back and told him how happy I was to hear that. I wanted to wake Madison, but knew she needed her rest. For Madison, this would be the best day yet.

When Madison woke up she asked about James. Seth was by her side and holding her hand. "He came through the surgery and they have him in the recovery room right now." Madison began blurting out, "I want to see him! I have to see him!" We will as soon as they give us permission to go in there. Madison had not remembered every detail of the wreck and was still somewhat in shock. Knowing her son would be fine and her friends and family were by her side, Madison began feeling more at ease.

"Hey sunshine," I said when I walked into Madison's room. It was 7:30 the next morning and none of us had really gotten any sleep. Madison's parents had gone home around midnight and would be returning soon. Ellie, Seth and I had decided to stay at the hospital. Ellie and I got to know Seth pretty well in the time we were together and we decided that we both liked him and are very excited he is marrying our best friend.

"I am so sore," Madison groaned. The nurse would be coming in soon to give Madison her meds. We gathered around her and talked to her for a bit and told her how well James had done through his surgery. Ellie told Madison and Seth that their son was a real trooper. They both smiled and Seth bent down to kiss Madison. He then said that he was putting in for a transfer immediately. "You all need me here." This made Madison smile and Ellie and I beamed at the news.

A tall handsome doctor came into the room and introduced himself. He was there to inform Seth and Madison that they could visit their son, but only for a brief time. I told Ellie if I wasn't married I would definitely be sinking my claws into Dr. Hottie. She laughed. We helped Madison sit up and Seth picked her up to put in her in the wheelchair. Ellie and I decided to go down to the hospital cafeteria to grab some breakfast and chat a while. We hugged Madison and made our way to the elevator. When we got in the elevator, Ellie and I both looked at each other and cracked up. Dr. Hottie was standing behind us in the elevator and Ellie knew I was about to lose it. Then she said, "It sure is warm in here."

When the doctor reached his floor and made his way out of the elevator, he gave Ellie and me a wink and we burst out laughing. I said, "Do you think he knew what we were up to?" Ellie said, "Of course he did, he is a doctor ya know." Ellie and I are trouble and we can't even behave in a hospital I said to myself. She must have read my mind because she looked at me and let out the biggest laugh. When we finally got to the cafeteria we noticed it was swarming with quite a few hot doctors. I told Ellie we had to behave or they would kick us out. She agreed. We ordered a platter of eggs and toast. After we paid for our food we walked over to the orange juice maker. A small line had formed and as we stood there we admired the nice sights that were among us. Ellie nudged me and said she was already getting over what's his face. I said, "Why do you say that?" She pointed and said, "I'm going to introduce myself to that gorgeous man before I leave this hospital." I laughed and all I could say was, "You go girl." I was glad to see that Ellie was learning how to be strong on her own.

Ellie was flirting with her body as she pretended to listen to me chatter about different things. I knew she was only half listening and I finally told her she needed to get up, go over to the handsome doctor she couldn't keep her eyes off and introduce herself. He wasn't wearing a ring so hopefully that meant he wasn't married.

"Huh, were you talking to me?" She said.

"Yes I am. Get up and go over there already."

"I can't," she said. "He's probably seeing someone."

"You will never know if you don't make the first move."

"Brooke, not now. I'm still getting over what's his face."

"You can't even remember his name," I reminded her.

"Brooke, he hurt me so bad and I can't go through that again!"

"He just wasn't the one for you."

She picked up a forkful of eggs and I said, "UH OH! You don't have to make the first move, he's on his way over here!" Ellie didn't even have time to swallow her eggs.

"Hello ladies," Dr. Hottie said.

Poor Ellie couldn't even talk because she was still chewing. Finish your eggs Ellie and do it now I screamed with my eyes. She went to speak but nothing came out. What a disaster.

"Hi, my name is Brooke," I said nonchalantly. And this is my best friend Ellie. And by the way she is single."

Ellie looked at me like she wanted to strangle me, but the nice looking doctor admired her and said REALLY? Ellie apologized for her friend being so forward and he laughed. He said it wasn't every day that you see two beautiful women in the hospital cafeteria. Was this a line? Probably. But if he asked Ellie out maybe it would help her get over that bum that did her so terribly wrong.

"My name is Ronald Williams, but people call me Ron." Ellie liked the name Ron and felt it fit him nicely. He told her his shift would be ending around 4 and he would like to talk to her some more if she would like to. Oh did she ever. He shook our hands and told her he would meet her in the front lobby of the hospital. She almost jumped out of her seat. I was so excited for her. As he walked away, we admired his backside. I poked her and told her she had the magic touch. Ellie looked at me and said thank you. I said, "What for?" She said, "For being you!"

We spent the day with Madison, Seth and James. James was weak, but we knew he was going to be fine. I told Madison when she and James were better we would have a get together at my house. Madison told me it may be a while before that happens, but I told her they would be back to normal before she knew it. James would be staying in the hospital a few more days than Madison, but they felt that he would be home by the middle of the week. Madison didn't want to leave him alone so she and Seth had made a pact that they would take turns sitting with him every day until he was released.

Around 3:00 I decided to go home and spend time with my family. I had missed them and wanted to prepare a nice dinner. I knew Madison would be fine with Seth by her side and Ellie sure didn't need me. In one short hour she would be in la la land with Dr. Ron. I smiled as I walked to the elevator and began thinking how different I would have been feeling if James or Madison wouldn't have been ok. I shuddered at the thought of that and looked up to thank God for His blessings that day. I was proud of myself because I truly was beginning to put all my faith in Him and knew that even the bleakest days are followed by His shining light.

Chapter 14

When I arrived home I noticed David was sitting alone and looking rather rough. "Hey hun, what's up?" I cheerfully asked. "Brooke, I need to tell you something," he quietly said. I wondered what in the world could he have to tell me. He didn't even ask how my best friend and son were, so whatever he had to say must have been pretty important. "Ok," I managed to say without sounding worried. "Come sit down with me," he said. As I walked over to where he was sitting I began to feel his tension. "David, are you alright?" I asked. He said he was fine, but had to come clean with me. Now that didn't sound good at all!

"Brooke, I haven't been a very decent person lately," he claimed.

"Honey, it's ok. I forgive you for the pictures you had on the computer.

"We have already been over this."

"That's not what I mean."

"Then what," I slowly asked.

"I....I've been seeing someone.

My face went pale and numbness ran over my body in an instant. "**NO, NO, NO!**" I screamed. "You would never do that to me, not you!" It was pure denial and I wouldn't believe it to be any other way. David went to reach for me and I began swinging. I was a complete maniac and he couldn't control me. I was frantic, my world just flipped upside down on me and everything that I knew to be true wasn't! I continued screaming and flailing until he was able to grab me and hold me tight. "Brooke, stop it, listen to me." The fight in me was strong but my muscles began aching.

"I love you Brooke and I always have. I was wrong, oh so wrong. Please don't leave me, please don't leave me." "**I HATE YOU DAVID ANDERSON! GET OUT!!!!!**" I screamed. But he wouldn't budge. He just sat there rocking me and crying. I didn't know what to do and I swear if I had a weapon in my hand I would have already used it on him. Please baby, please forgive me is what he kept saying over and over and over. How could I? For better or worse were the words shouting in my mind, but I tried so desperately to block it out. Why wouldn't those words stop screaming in my head. I couldn't do anything but cry on his shoulder. My marriage was an implausible mess and I didn't think any good could come from this.

We held onto each other for what seemed an eternity. I couldn't move. My legs had turned to jelly and all I could do was shake and cry. He had been my everything and now all I wanted to do was run and hide from him. His touch was no longer golden to me. His touch had become tainted and the sight of him made me want to scream more. The hands he had wrapped so tightly around me were the same hands that caressed another woman's body. The eyes I looked into held the stare of another woman. What we had shared for so long now belonged to someone else. "Let go of me!" I screamed one last time. He loosened his hands from me and I broke free. I ran to our bedroom and frantically began throwing his belongings in the opened suitcase I had thrown on the bed. Once it was closed I took it and threw it at him. "Don't ever come back!" I shouted.

David slowly picked up the suitcase, walked to the door and told me he would never stop loving me. I told him it was too late he already had. I was left standing a few feet from the front door and my legs gave out. I fell in a heap and cried so hard that I figured my body would explode. I had never cried that hard in all my life and felt like the best part of me had died that afternoon. What was I going to do? This I kept saying to myself until I couldn't anymore. What would I tell the girls? They were old enough where I couldn't lie. They were aware of adultery. How could the love of my life destroy me in this way? Was our marriage that bad that he had to step out on me? I had no one to talk to. Madison was trying to recuperate and Ellie was meeting what could be her future husband and I'm lying here with the world caving in on me. I couldn't talk to David. Not now and maybe not ever. I got up, went to my room, fell on the bed and began crying some more.

It was 7:00 and my phone was ringing. It was David. Hell no, I said to myself. I have nothing more to say. So I sat and listened to the phone ring endlessly. I didn't care if he did this the rest of the evening. I didn't have to listen to him whine that he shouldn't have done this to me. It happened and as far as I knew our marriage was done. You committed the ultimate sin David I thought to myself and you will have to suffer as you are making me. Even though I was trying to make myself believe I didn't need him, a big part of me did. But for now that part of me that wanted him had to be ignored.

The girls were out for the evening and I was grateful for that. I didn't want them to see the wreck that I had become. I didn't know what I was going to tell them. Maybe I would just say that their dad and I were spending some time apart. Or maybe I would just tell them what he did to me. He was the one who did wrong, but I felt so sad about sharing that with them. I had to talk to someone so I decided to call Ellie. I wondered if she was still with Dr. Ron.

"Hello," Ellie said in a quite cheerful voice.

All I could manage to say was "Ellie!"

"Brooke, what is it? What's the matter? You don't sound right."

"David......he-he-he cheated on me!" I said before I began to lose it.

"WHAT?" Ellie shouted. Ellie had to know all the details.

"Brooke, can I come over?"

I needed fresh air so I told her I would like to get out because I was suffocating in my house. We decided to meet at the park. I was a mess, but

I knew hearing children's laughter would ease my pain. We decided to meet right away.

"Oh Brooke, I don't know what to say. "I don't either." I couldn't believe that I began telling her what happened without crying. Sure we were going through a rough patch, but I had no idea it would lead to this. "Why did he do this to me?" Ellie just sat there staring at the ground. She couldn't answer any questions because she had been through the same thing with her ex. and with Michael.

"Brooke, maybe David was just going through a rough time and made a mistake. It's not like he's ever done this before and from what you are telling me he seems so very sorry for what he did."

"Are you kidding me? I'm to feel sorry for what he did to me, what he did to our marriage. No way!"

"I know how you feel, but somehow this whole thing may be a blessing in disguise."

Had my best friend lost her mind? "And why do you say that?" I asked.

"Well, maybe it took something this bad for him to realize that he could never live without you. Maybe he had been doubting it for some time, but this situation made him become a better man for you."

"Are you insane?" I screamed. He wanted his cake and to eat it too. It's as simple as that!" Why was she justifying what he had done? How could she not be on my side at a time like this?

"What about Jason and what he did to you?" I angrily said. Man, I shouldn't have dug that hole, but she needed to make me understand where she was coming from. "Jason was different. He loved the idea of having a wife and kids, but he wasn't in love with me. Sure I thought he was the real deal, but when I kicked him out he told me I was doing him a real favor. All I'm doing is comparing what he said to what David said and I'm trying to get you to see that my dirt bag ex husband didn't even care that our marriage was going to end. Hell he actually welcomed it. But David, he's different. He was weak and went too far. Yes what he did and keeping it from you is hardly forgivable, but he seems very genuine about his mistake." I didn't want to listen to Ellie, but knew that what she was saying made a lot of sense.

"What am I going to do, Ellie?" I will never be able to trust him again. "Brooke, I can't tell you what to do. I can only tell you to go with what your heart is telling you." Right now my heart was broken and couldn't talk. As we sat there watching a few children running around with no cares in the world, Ellie began telling me about the rendevouz she had with Michael at the park. She told me he was just a guy to help her get over Jason and she was beginning to realize it. Just the evening before had he ended it with her and she thought her world was over. She realized now that there are many more things in life that are important and that her being in a serious relationship wasn't what she needed right now. She told me that Michael too had been a married man and that if he wouldn't have ended it, she would have. I began thinking how much Ellie and I actually had in common.

We stayed at the park until the first hint of night appeared. Ellie asked me if I would be ok. I told her I had a lot to think about when I got home. Ellie understood. Before we parted ways, Ellie gave me a hug and told me to call her if I needed to talk. I was so drained that I probably wouldn't even stay up to think things over. Last night and today were enough tragic for a lifetime and maybe it was best for me to just get a good night's rest. On the way home the radio was playing our song and the tears were unstoppable. I didn't know how to go on without David in my life. I didn't want to live with him, but I didn't know how to live without him. When I arrived home I made a bee line to my bedroom and crashed on what used to be our bed. Now it was my bed and I felt so alone.

The next morning was dreadful. No David by my side and knowing I had to tell our daughter's why their dad isn't home was not something that I particularly wanted to do. David is the one who messed everything up so why isn't he here to explain it? Maybe that's what I need to do, call David and have him help me explain to the girls why their dad isn't living at home. All this was just too much. This is not something I thought I would ever have to face. Oh David, were you even thinking about the potential problems that would come along with you having an affair? Of course you didn't! Before I walked to the kitchen I could feel the tears welling up in my eyes and I knew that talking to our daughters was something I couldn't do by myself. No, David would have to come over and we would all sit down and have a family meeting. Too bad if he didn't want to because this time he didn't have a chance to get out of it! I finally got up the nerve to call David.

"Hello," David said.

"David, I need you to come over. You need to help me explain to the girls why you aren't here."

"Brooke, do you want me to tell them the truth? Don't you think that will turn out to be disasterous?" He asked.

"David, we don't need to lie to them and you should have thought about that before you started sneaking around with another woman."

My head was splitting and I knew an ulcer had to be forming in my stomach. "Can we just tell them that we are having problems and taking some time apart?" He begged. He was desperate and I shouldn't have felt sorry for him, but I did for some strange reason. "Brooke, please know that what I did was unspeakable and I really don't know why I did it." "Did you love her?" I cried. "No. She was more like a good friend," he said. A good friend that you shared your body with!" He grew quiet and then said, "I've never loved anyone like you and never will and I don't know what else to say.....I really don't!"

Although I didn't want to go along with what he wanted to tell the girls, I agreed. I had to stay strong and not give into his sadness, but I really didn't want the girls to hate their own father. As I made my way to the kitchen, I noticed that no one else was awake. I was thankful for that. David would be over shortly and I really didn't know how I was going to react to his presence. I really had to control the anger that was rushing through my body. I am going to be the better person. I won't allow hate to take over. I didn't know what the outcome was going to be. I just knew that faith is all I had to rely on.

When I heard the knock on the door I knew it had to be David. My heart sunk and I even began feeling shaky. I slowly opened the front door and noticed immediately how bad David looked. He looked as if he hadn't slept all night. Pure pitiful is how you could sum up the way he looked. But I wouldn't feel sorry for this at all. He stood frozen, staring at me with a tired gaze in his eyes. "Come in David. The girls aren't awake yet, but you can come in the kitchen and help me make breakfast." He agreed and walked slowly to the kitchen. "Brooke, I really want to talk to you about all this," he wailed.

"David, PLEASE!!!!! I am trying to be calm, but talking about the details of your lovemaking with another woman will not allow me to stay calm. So please don't tell me you want to talk about any of this."

"Alright," he managed to say.

The aromas from the meal must have awaken the girls because they all found their way to the kitchen. I wanted the girls to enjoy their breakfast before they had to be involved with our troubles. Danielle and Ashlei didn't seem to notice that there was anything out of the ordinary, but Noelle could sense that something was different so she spoke up right away.

"Hey dad, why do you look so bad?" She asked. I wondered how he was going to reply to that one. He just gave her a quirky smile and told her that after breakfast we had to talk to them. Noelle didn't say anything, but looked perplexed. Breakfast this morning was unusually quiet and that was a first. Meal time in the Anderson home was normally anything but quiet. But this morning was not a normal morning. The girls were busily eating their eggs and grits, but I couldn't eat. My stomach was in knots and I thought to myself this may be the last time we sit in this kitchen as a family. "So, why is everyone so quiet?" Danielle asked. No one replied. She left it alone and continued eating. I couldn't look at David because when I did all I could think about was him with his arms wrapped around another woman. A sea of anger, frustration, disgust and pain welled through my soul and I didn't know if it would ever stop. I had been cut to the bone and was left in pure misery. David would never know how bad that felt. He couldn't.

When everyone was finished eating their breakfast, David called his family into the living room for a family talk. The girls looked at each other with concern and knew this was not a good sign. They each took a seat while David and I stood in the center of the room.

"Girls, we have something to tell you," David said.

"Mom's not pregnant, is she?"Noelle asked.

"Nothing like that Noelle," I explained. David seemed lost for words at this point so I intercepted. Your dad and I are taking a break from each other for a while. David looked down at the carpet as if it were going to give him some magic words to use to make everything alright. "Why?" Ashlei asked. At this point of the conversation, David admitted to having an affair because he knew it was the right thing to do even if it meant his girls would despise him for the rest of his life. They sat there in shock and Danielle told him to get out. "You aren't welcomed here anymore!" She screamed. I knew I had to keep it together for the sake of the girls and this was not the time for me to fall apart. David slowly walked toward the door feeling the weight of the world on him. Before he left he turned around to tell his family he was sorry and he would always love them. But this is not what the Anderson girls wanted to hear. They had turned deaf ears on him the minute he proclaimed his unfaithfulness. I stood there with empty emotions and feeling so helpless. The life our family had was stained forever. Our girls came to be by my side and even though I really disliked my husband right now, the only thing I wanted at this very moment was his strong arms to be wrapped around our family while telling us that everything was going to be just fine.

David drove back to the hotel he had been staying at and felt awful pangs of guilt throughout his body. Everything he loved and knew was gone. Or was it? Could he fix this terrible thing he had done to Brooke and his girls? Would they ever give him another chance in this lifetime? He would return to the crappy room he had just begun occupying and think of all the different ways he could win them back. He was truly sorry and this mistake would be one that he would never make again as long as he lived. Brooke and the girls just needed time he thought to himself. Time was what he would give them. A stupid short winded affair was not going to destroy his family, not at all. It was fixable and he was sure of that. Now all he had to do was figure out how to convince his wife and daughters to take him back.

Once I convinced the girls that I was going to be fine I made my way up the stairs and into the bathroom. I longed to take a nice relaxing bath and thought I deserved it. I told myself I could sit in pity or I could find strength and try to move on. I decided that I would be like Brooke and Madison and search for the strength I knew I had deep within me. David would have to live in sadness and regret, why should I? I wasn't sure what tomorrow was going to bring, but I knew that whatever it was I was going to be prepared to face it.

Chapter 15

Ellie was worried about Madison and Brooke so she decided to call Brooke and ask her if she wanted to visit Madison at the hospital. She figured she could spread some cheer their way. Ellie was grateful to hear that Madison and James were doing much better and would be leaving the hospital in a couple of days. She wasn't sure about Brooke though. The pain she was going through might take months or years to disintegrate. Ellie knew that all too well.

"Mom, your friend is on the phone and would like to talk to you," shouted Noelle. "Who is it Noelle?" I asked. "Ellie," she replied. "Tell her I will call her back shortly." As I lay there relaxing in the warm water my thoughts began swirling around in my head. Thoughts of how happy I had been just a short week ago. The flowers and the sweet talking and the over affectionate husband had all been a way for David to feel better about what he had done. A pure idiot I had been all along. But now he seemed so remorseful. I would have to make him suffer for what he did and maybe get in touch with a well know therapist. For now, I was going to focus on myself and the girls and only time would tell if our marriage was going to make it or not.

Once I got dressed and blow dried my hair I decided to call Ellie back. Talking to her would take my mind off all this crazy havoc . "Hey Ellie," I managed to say in the most upbeat voice that I could find. "Brooke, I wanted to know if you would like to visit Madison and James in a little bit?"

"I'd love to," I said. We talked a few more minutes and then I told Ellie that if I didn't get off the phone I would never be ready to go. My mind was now focused on other things and this was how I needed it to be for my own sanity. As I got ready, I thought about how life always had surprises and that it truly was best to take one day at a time. I would find this thinking to be positive and decided to make it my new mantra.

I would begin looking on the bright side and even consider doing some real soul searching. I began to feel better about my life and thought this was a good start to a new day. I actually began to smile while I began looking at myself in the mirror. I was still a very attractive woman and decided at that very moment that whatever drove my husband to do what he did had nothing to do with my weight or my age. A pitfall in life had blindsided us and somehow we would go on. Only time would tell if we would go on together.

Ellie arrived just as I was finishing putting my clothes on. I told her to come on in and make herself comfortable. It was going to be a wonderful day I told myself as I looked one last time in the mirror. I knew Madison would be so happy to see us and I hoped she would be feeling better. Hopefully Ellie and I could make her laugh. Poor Madison had been through the ringer and she needed some comic relief.

As I made my way into the living room I couldn't help but notice the horrified look on Ellie's face as she stood holding one of our family pictures. Her eyes were glued to the picture and my calling her name didn't phase her one bit. "Ellie, what is it?" I asked. "Ellie answer me!" "What is the matter?" I urgently requested. She seemed to be muttering something over and over, but for the life of me I couldn't figure out what she was saying. "Ellie, you are scaring me." At that, she looked up and said in a faint whisper, "It can't be." What can't be? What is she mumbling about? I walked over to her and noticed her pointing to David. I began thinking that he must resemble someone she knew and it brought her bad memories. She turned her eyes from the picture to me and burst out into a crying fit. Whatever made her react like this was freaking me out. I didn't know how to calm her so I waited for the tears to stop. After ten minutes of her sobbing and shaking uncontrollably, she finally managed to say Michael. Michael, why would she say his name? Oh no, maybe David reminded her of Michael. But why would she be so upset? Just the other day she shared with me that Michael was becoming a faint memory in her mind. Nothing was making sense. "Ellie, you are not making any sense. Sit down and tell me what is going on." I helped her to the couch, picture still in hand and once again calmly asked her to tell me why she was so upset.

Oh Brooke is all she could say. "Honey, what is it? You can tell me." "I am so sorry, I am so sorry, I am so sorry!" She replied. Why? "It's him," she exclaimed. I sat there a few minutes and sudden fear flooded me. I was beginning to solve a puzzle. And Ellie was handing me the last piece to that puzzle. Pointing to David, saying I'm sorry, mentioning Michael's name, and saying it's him only meant one thing.

My David was her Michael. Her Michael was my......DAVID! My body went numb, I lost my breath, and my mind escaped me. Say something were the words pounding in my head when I slowly came back to reality. Tell me what I'm thinking is so not true. But Ellie didn't say anything. A flood of fear overcame me and I wanted to vanish from this spot in my living room. My best friend in the whole world was getting ready to tell me something that I knew would probably be the worst news of all. Now it was my moment to find out what I didn't want to know, but needed to know. "Ellie, the man you are pointing to is my husband," I hysterically said. She shook her head continuously and cried out, "No, this is Michael!" I feared the worst and couldn't predict what my next action would be. I took the picture from her weak hands and threw it across the room. I screamed and thought that if I was ever close to having a break down this was it. The glass smashed into what seemed to be a million pieces when it hit the hardwood floor and I fell to my knees. My world had caved in on me and I was buried under a ton of rubble. Ellie knelt down to my side and in my most hateful voice I told her to get out of my house and to never ever come back. She broke down and I didn't care. How would I ever accept what my best friend had done with my husband? Ellie slowly made her way to the door and couldn't stop telling me how sorry she was and how much she still loved me and didn't know what she would do without our friendship. I refused to look at her. At this point I really didn't think I could ever forgive Ellie or my husband for what they had done to me.

I lay on the living room floor for what seemed a few hours. I couldn't move and stayed in a frozen fetal position. I thought my life was surely over. First David coming clean, then Ellie. This was all too much for me to deal with. With the small amount of strength that I had left in me, I reached for the phone and hit the number (on speed dial) that belonged to my husband who had been, in all reality, leading a double life. At that moment, I began thinking about the name Michael. This name was the one his mother wanted to give him before he was born, but his father wouldn't agree to it. He had told me the story in the early years of our marriage when we were trying to decide on names for our children. That sly son of a bitch! If he was here right now, he would be paying dearly. Oh, David (Michael) whoever the hell you claim to be, you better pick up your phone and start explaining yourself right now!!!

"Hello", David said. My voice froze when I went to speak. "Brooke, is that you?" He slowly asked.

"You arrogant, son of a bitch!" I shouted.

"Brooke, what is it?" He asked.

"You tell me, David or should I say Michael," I screamed.

David tried to play dumb and wondered how in God's green earth Brooke came to know that piece of his secret. Oh yea David, I know all about your fake name and who you were romping around with. David kept quiet because he didn't know what to say. **My best friend, David!** Of all the women you had to fool around with, you choose my best friend!

Chapter 16

Of all the damndest, stupidest things he had done in his lifetime this had to top them all! He wasn't the type to screw up to this extreme. David was coming to the realization that he would be facing a divorce, a tumultuous one at that and there was probably nothing he could say or do to win back the love of his life. Now he would fit in the category of bachelor for life, living off of beanie weenies and residing in a one bedroom apartment and if he was lucky maybe a friend or two would eventually swing by to visit. He doubted that though because when this news leaked out he would be the laughing stalk of the town. He also knew that if his daughters ever forgave him they may call or text him with a simple hello and leave it at that-maybe, but that he seriously doubted!

David put his head in his hands and began to weep. He would never forgive himself for giving into evil temptations. He knew Brooke couldn't even begin to understand what it was like for a man to experience the struggles that related to the weakness of the flesh that he was sure all men had to deal with from time to time. This indeed was the scariest feeling that he thinks he has ever experienced in his entire life. Brooke had been with him the majority of his life and she was all he knew. She and the girls were what brought him comfort and kept him grounded. How could a few months of blinded lust cause him his life? He had destroyed a marriage and the close friendship his wife had shared with Ellie. He went to pick the phone up, but decided against it. What was the point in that? Brooke wouldn't take this call or any calls from him today or ever. Any conversation would be directed to his lawyer.

Ellie was shaking so badly that she knew if she didn't pull over she would end up in a wreck and she knew she couldn't cause anymore harm to anyone else. She did just that. Ellie struggled to breathe and knew a panic attack was coming on. This is what she deserved she told herself. If only she could have been a better wife to Jason her meeting David would have never happened. She was such a failure at life. And she was now minus a best friend because she made the worst mistake ever. She wanted to rip every hair out of Michael's head because of the pain he put Brooke through. He was merely a wolf in sheep's clothing and everyone suffered because of it. Ellie knew that she was banned from Brooke for life and the only thing she knew to do at this point was to pull herself together, get back on the highway and head to Madison's house. Madison was the only one she felt she could confide in and was confident that Madison would look at this situation objectively.

Madison and James had been recovering nicely, but were still a little sore. Madison was in good spirits because Seth would be receiving his transfer by the following week and they would be a family soon. The pieces of her life were finally falling into place for James and her. Florida was the best decision she had made. A new job, a changed man and a wonderful son, who was healing nicely, were the best gifts she could ever receive. She knew money couldn't buy those precious things. The vibration of her phone pulled her away from her thoughts. She picked her phone up and said hello.

"Mad-i-son," wailed Ellie.

"What?"

"Is that you Ellie?

Ellie broke down and asked if Madison could possibly allow her to come over for a bit. "Of course you can come over." Ellie thanked her but worried that once Madison found out what she was responsible for there may be one more lost friendship. Ellie blamed herself even though she hadn't known he was married. Somehow the clues that he was married to her best friend had to be there all along so how could she have missed them? As Ellie drove slowly, her thoughts ran away from her quickly. If she knew where Michael was at this time she would probably kill him. Thank God she had no idea where he was staying. As she turned into Madison's neighborhood, she gripped the steering wheel hard and told herself to calm down. She hoped James was sleeping or over at his grandparents so he didn't have to be exposed to all of her issues. She trembled as she went to knock on the door and prayed that she didn't have a breakdown on Madison's front porch.

Madison came to the door and couldn't believe how distressed Ellie looked. Madison questioned Ellie right away and Ellie was lost for words because her mind was blank. For some odd reason all she could picture was sitting at Angelina's with her two best friends in the whole world. God, she wished that's where she was right now enjoying laughs and drinks like old times.

"Ellie, Ellie, ELLIE! Hello," Madison was shouting.

"Hmmmm......"What?" Ellie asked. Once again Ellie had escaped reality and Madison was doing her best to snap her back into it.

Oh, Madison, I have done something that is so unforgiveable. Once these words left Ellie's tongue, she began to break down in hysteria and Madison didn't know how to even comfort her best friend. "Ellie, whatever you have done, I am sure you can be forgiven. Now calm down and tell me what in the world is going on." Madison's confusion had her perplexed and she didn't like feeling that way. But Madison was the analyzer and knew that all problems, no matter how big or small, always had a solution.

After about ten minutes of steady sobbing and rambling, Ellie finally blurted out—"I HAVE BEEN SLEEPING WITH DAVID THESE PAST FEW MONTHS!" Madison had only known of one David and that David belonged to Brooke. With this, Madison took a deep breath and a step back. Her mouth dropped open and her mind was racing with confusion. Ellie continued rambling phrases like: he lied to me, I didn't know, it was a game to him, my best friend hates me, I'm a failure and so on.

"Ellie, what in the world have you done?" Madison demanded to know. Ellie looked like a lunatic. She had lost all sense of reality and Madison didn't know whether to hug Ellie or deck her. How could Ellie have been sleeping with David and not know that he was Brooke's husband? Nothing was making sense. For God's sake the two of them worked together and were so close.

Ellie knew she would have to start from the beginning to help Madison understand the entirety of this Shakespearean drama. Madison told Ellie to start from the beginning and to not leave any details out. She was the crime scene investigator and this is how she approached life. Details, details, details-she knew were the key elements in solving crimes and life's complications.

"Well," Ellie began. It all started when I met Michael online. But it really wasn't Michael, it was David- Brooke's hus- Ellie couldn't get the rest of the word out and began to break down again. Madison was no dummy, she could clearly see how this disasterous situation began. "Oh Ellie, I told you online dating was a bad idea!" Ellie agreed and said, "What are the chances that of all the men who are online that I would choose to chat with the one man who was married to my best friend?" Madison then replied, "Slim to none, but it happened and now you have to somehow make Brooke see that you had no idea who you were really chatting with." Ellie decided that what Madison was saying was in fact the best advice she knew she could receive.

"Ellie, it wasn't your fault that you fell for a man without knowing he was living a double life. And if you had figured out that Michael really was David you would have ended it and told Brooke what her husband had been doing." What Madison was telling her made sense and Ellie began feeling a little better, but for some strange reason the pangs of guilt were still there.

"Madison, why did this happen?" Ellie asked sadly.

"Maybe it's a test of your friendship."

Ellie, how did you go on for two months and not one time introduce Michael to Brooke or me? This was the question that was circling in Madison's mind the whole time. So she blurted that question out for Ellie to hear. "Funny, you ask that because if he wouldn't have broken it off with me, I was going to introduce him to you all," Ellie responded. Madison hadn't even known that they weren't together until today. She really had been out of the loop. It almost seemed like a year had passed since the three friends had really been together to catch up on the important things.

"So Ellie, what are you going to do?" Ellie had calmed down and talking with a rational person helped. She looked at Madison and said, "I have no idea and that's why I came to you." This made Madison feel good, but she was used to being the advice slayer. She wondered if being a psychologist was what her career choice should have been.

Madison knew she had to act fast because an important friendship was at sake and she even wondered if Brooke would ever forgive Ellie. Brooke was very stubborn and didn't always see the real side of situations. Instead she seemed to transform a situation into the version that made sense to her and allowed emotions to disguise reality. Madison didn't understand that because solving problems mixed with emotions wasn't a good combination at all. Never let emotions get in the way of problem solving. A realistic person knew that.

"What if I call Brooke over right now and we have an intervention, if you will?" Madison asked.

"No way! Brooke would never agree to that," Ellie screamed.

Madison looked at Ellie and laughed. "Girl, Brooke is angry beyond belief, I'm sure, but don't give up just yet."

Ellie wanted so badly to see Brooke and make things right again, but knew it was still too soon. She knew Brooke and Brooke needed a lot of time before she could be in the same room as Ellie. Ellie told Madison that she wasn't going to bother Brooke that day and the poor girl probably needed a lot more time to figure out what she needed to do. The last thing Brooke needed was to see her husband's mistress and ex best friend.

Chapter 17

I managed to peel myself off the living room floor and carefully avoided getting splinters of glass in my bare feet. I stood stiff looking at the shattered pieces of glass and thought to myself how much those shiny speckles had once been molded together to hold a beloved picture of my past, but now that same glass had become tiny, broken pieces of trash to be discarded. That is exactly how my marriage to David and friendship to Ellie was now. I was frantic with fear because all I seemed to have now was myself. Our kids were practically adults and never home, Madison was getting married and starting a whole new life, and there could be no more David and Ellie. I couldn't cry anymore because the strength had diminished and the well was dried up. I felt my life had ended. As I stood with millions of emotions stirring within me, I noticed my phone was displaying a new text message. I looked at it and decided to read it. It said: Brooke, Please find it in your heart to forgive me. I made a huge mistake and will always love you. 02/16/91.

I couldn't take it. My anger took over quickly and I threw the phone across the room. I didn't even care if it broke. Why did he have to add the date we had taken those solemn vows? I mean the date I took those solemn vows? What a mockery he had made of me I thought to myself. My loneliness and anger were too much to bear and I knew that emotions had to stop guiding me and it was time that I lead my life with intelligent decisions. Once a cheater, always a cheater I began telling myself over and over.

Our dirty laundry had traveled fast in our small community, but that was no surprise at all. I didn't care because I wanted so badly for people to see who the real David Anderson truly was. A scorned woman hath much revenge! I had never really been the type of person that believed in an eye for an eye, but David had made me bitter and it was now on him. He would look like the fool, not me. As for Ellie, the rumor didn't include her name. I wasn't really that evil. Not yet anyway. I was adjusting to my new life (if you want to call it that), but had only been living off of junk food and remorse. Not a great way to live, but this was my way of dealing so people left me alone and let me deal. David called every day this past week but I refused to answer. I also refused to listen to his pathetic voicemail messages too and found myself deleting every single one of them. The ass didn't deserve any of my time. Hahaha! You sorry son of a bitch! Now let's see how life without booty is for you these days. No woman would want him after the stunt he pulled (or so I thought anyway).

Gabby was busily plotting how she could sink her claws into the newly separated David. She knew that Brooke wouldn't care and this would be a perfect opportunity for her to snatch up that good looking man who she had dreamed about so very often. She knew deep down that his marriage to that goody-goody Brooke was disintegrating. Finally, with Brooke out of the picture, she could have a decent shot at love or something close to that. Gabby had never had luck at love, but somehow she had a good feeling about this one. She wasn't a bad looking woman and she knew David was the type that wanted a good looking trophy wife to stand by his side. She was confident in her looks because she had often seen men staring at her when she was out and about. She would catch their glares and it would feed her ego. She was so ready for a man to love her. David seemed to know about love and lust and yes that should have been a red flag for her, but she was lonely and a fun time was what she wanted now. Love would come later if it was in the cards for her.

Gabby had a sneaky suspicion that David would be coming into her flower shop very soon. He was like any other man who bought flowers for their wives and girlfriends when they screwed up. If he didn't come into her shop, she would have to find him. Either way, she knew that her life was going to get very interesting very soon.

Just as Gabby had predicted, David entered her shop later that week. David looked like hell. He seemed to have aged five years she thought, but he still looked sexy and distinguished. A week had passed and David wasn't sleeping, eating or working much. He was living with tremendous guilt that had seemed to be eating him from the inside out. Brooke had always loved flowers and although he knew his chances of being with her were gone, he believed flowers would at least brighten her day.

"Hello there, Cowboy," came that familiar voice from behind the counter. "Hey Gabby, how's it going?" David asked.

His personal hell was going to be an advantage to her and she had to smile. Yes, she should have felt bad for him, but why would she when it created such an awesome opportunity for her? She would make it all better for him anyway and once he spent a night with her he would totally forget about Brooke. Fate was now handing her what she had deserved all along and she was not going to let this one get away.

Gabby pranced from behind the counter and David couldn't help but notice how happy she was, but then again everyone was happier than him. She told him how pitiful he looked and told him that the stress he had was showing. So she began massaging his tense shoulders. David tried to resist her touch, but he was too weak and began to enjoy the extra attention she was showing him. God, it had been a long time since Brooke had given him attention like that.

"Oh Gabby, that feels so damn good," he said. Gabby smiled a devilish grin and thought this was too easy. As she rubbed, she began making small talk. She never really did like silence. As she assumed, David didn't have much to say, but she carried on conversation anyway. David had welcomed any conversation because lately no one had called him, not even his best friend Tom. Tom's wife had such a short leash on him and David figured Tom wasn't allowed to call or visit him after what he had done to Brooke.

Gabby didn't really feel like creating a beautiful floral arrangement that David was going to request, but knew small talk could only go so far and she was running a legitimate business so she quit massaging David's shoulders and asked him if he wanted the same as usual. He smiled and told her that's why he kept coming to her. She did a great job every time and he counted on her for that. **David, David, David!** She screamed inside her head- wake up and smell the coffee. You and Brooke are over baby and these stupid flowers aren't going to mend your broken marriage! What was it with men anyway? They always seemed to think that flowers heal everything.

"So, I guess you have heard the latest gossip about Brooke and me," David gloomily said.

"Well sweetie, this is a small town and people do talk," Gabby plainly said.

David had always felt at ease talking to Gabby. She was so much like the sister he never had. His chest started relaxing because Gabby had made him feel such at ease. He was the one who brought it up, not her. Most women wouldn't even want to give him the time of day because of the wicked thing he had done, but Gabby was so different.

"Gabby, I really messed up this time. I ruined my 20 year marriage to the best woman in the world, my relationship with my daughters, and probably my business. I am a fool and don't know where to go from here." Gabby then blurted out: "David, do you still love her after what you did to her?" He replied, "Of course I do, she is the love of my life and I will never stop loving her." Gabby sank when she heard that and hoped the despair wasn't showing on her face. She began thinking that there may be a small chance that Brooke may soften and decide to take David back. He would never stray again after the mistake he had made. Gabby had to grab her chance to be with him so she decided to act fast! She knew it was now time to end this conversation and put herself first.

"Hey, David it won't take me that long to arrange these flowers and I will be closing up soon. How bout you and I go grab a drink and bite to eat?"

"Gabby, I don't know," he replied.

"Come on, we are old friends and old friends have to eat ya know! Besides you don't want to be alone and I don't want to be alone so let's take advantage of the time we have and go sink sorrows where they belong- in a nice cold drink."

David laughed and realized that was the first time he had laughed in about a month. Nothing in his life had made him happy enough to laugh and he decided that spending time with an old friend was exactly what he needed. Little did he know that Gabby had an agenda of her own.

"Ok, Miss Thing, let's blow this joint and have a laugh or two," he commented.

Gabby couldn't believe how easy it was to make this man feel so good. What the hell was wrong with his wife of twenty years to not have figured out how to make him feel this way. Brooke, baby you had your chance and you really blew it. No wonder he strayed. Gabby could feel his pain and believed what he had done was totally justifiable. Gabby was so lost in her thoughts she hadn't heard David talking to her. "I'm sorry Dave, did you say something?"

"Yea, I was wondering how much I owe you because I noticed your prices went up."

"You, my dear, can have them for free." David couldn't believe how generous Gabby was being, but of course he had no idea what her motives were. He hugged her and told her there needed to be more people in the world like her. Men, she decided, were so easy to manipulate especially when they were hurting. She knew her chances were now better than ever and she was floating on cloud nine.

She decided that taking two separate cars to the sports bar would be the best thing to do. She didn't want him to suspect any motives, not yet anyway. As she followed him, she began thinking to herself what kind of lover he would be. She giggled and told herself to stop wondering and find out already. She was naughty, but didn't care. Maybe tonight would be the best time to find that out. She wouldn't feel guilty because David was a free man and she sure didn't see Brooke coming to her senses. When she entered the parking lot she noticed David had been waiting for her and he actually seemed to look happy. This made her feel great. She knew how to bring out his happiness and that was very crucial at this moment in his life.

They walked in together and Gabby had made David laugh once again. This girl was a comedian he told himself. Laughter was the best medicine and she knew just how much of a dosage he needed. When they were seated, his eyes met hers and that sad, longing feeling came back to him quickly. He wondered what Brooke was doing and missed her so much. His heart wanted to shatter all over again. Yes, he enjoyed feeling young again when Ellie entered his life, but nothing really could compare to all the wonderful things his marriage had brought to him over the years- NOTHING! Ellie had been sweet and good for him as he struggled with life, but he should have gone to Brooke with these struggles and not to a stranger he met online.

Gabby knew David was buried deep in thought, but she decided to steal his attention. She began chatting about how life was hard and how she wished he could be happy. As they began drinking, Gabby and David became lost in the past sharing funny stories of their younger days. Gabby and the three drinks he consumed had been the perfect way to help David take his mind off of his wretched life. About an hour and a half later, Gabby's boldness took over. "Alright, David the night won't be complete until you come over to my place for a night cap," she blurted out. David was feeling really good now and he thanked the alcohol for that. He laughed and said, "Why not?"

David paid the bill because Gabby had been so kind to him for everything and off they went David to his car and Gabby to hers. They were only a few blocks from her place and they weren't drunk, just a little buzzed. David kept telling himself that being with a good old friend is just what he needed even if it was a female. He was tired of being sad and had lost almost all hope that Brooke would ever take him back. When they walked into her place he had decided that Gabby had done very well for herself. He knew that love had not been kind to her and he was happy that she could at least provide for herself and buy the nice things she wanted. As they sat down on her comfortable leather couch, David complimented her place and told her how proud he was that she had provided so nicely for herself. Gabby grew with such excitement because she knew men liked independent women. Thank you God or fate for providing me with this opportunity, she prayed quickly in her head and smiled. This was going to be the best night yet and it was long overdue.

Gabby moved a little closer to David and flirtatiously laughed as he began recapping an event from high school- an event that didn't include Brooke. She decided now was the time to tell him that she had been totally head over heels for him in high school. So she gained her confidence and started to explain to him that when she was in tenth grade she had a huge crush on him. She began to laugh and to her surprise David told her that she should have told him because he just might have asked her out. Gabby was at a loss for words and decided that this was her cue to make her move. She knew she could waste no more precious time. She began unbuttoning her blouse and whispered soft words into his ear. "Well David, we aren't in high school any more but you have your second chance tonight to be with me," she quietly said. He was shocked that a friendly outing was becoming so risky. He had drunk too much and lust had him in a tight hold. She was an attractive woman he had decided, but she was not Brooke. What the hell was he doing with Gabby? He was just her friend and that is how he wanted it to stay. He needed Brooke now and had to see her. His head was spinning and he didn't want to upset Gabby, but he couldn't continue being with other women.

"David, do I look hotter now than I did in high school?" Gabby seductively asked. David guessed the alcohol was making her act this way because Gabby was too sweet to have plotted these kinds of moves. He didn't want to hurt her feelings because she had been so kind to him so he told her yes she did and then he added, but you aren't Broo......He couldn't get her name out of his mouth because Gabby had already put her nice, smooth, warm lips on his. She didn't want to hear that name. Not tonight. So she pretended as if she didn't know what he said and she began kissing him in the most passionate way. Gabby felt dirty and sexy and this gave her fuel for her fire. She began touching him in dangerous places and David knew this wasn't good but once again the devil was egging him on to stay with her tonight. He wanted to be with a woman so badly. The euphoria was becoming too much for him as she was beginning to please him. This girl moved fast—too fast for him. She climbed on top of him and David froze. This moment was so intense and he was excited, ashamed, and confused all at same time. "Gabby........ Come on girl. We can't do this. I am still a married man." Gabby refused to listen and thought that maybe if she slowed down a bit he would calm down and quit talking that nonsense. She climbed off his lap and began dancing, almost in a striptease kind of way.

David began pulling himself back into reality and decided to do what he should have when she started throwing herself at him. He got up from the couch and slowly walked toward her. Gabby liked this. She just knew that he wanted to dance with her so she pulled him closer to her. David must have been sending her mixed signals and he hated himself for that, but he had to get out of her apartment and fast. He refused to go down this path once again and make the same mistake twice. He pushed her away and told her he was sorry, but he wasn't ready for a new woman and he had to make things right with Brooke.

"David, your marriage is over! It's time you have fun and I am willing to be the one you have fun with. Please stay with me and I will give you the most memorable night ever," she pleaded. David stood there feeling sorry for her and didn't want to end up single, alone and desperate like Gabby had been for so many years. He apologized and made a beeline for her door. She was enraged and told him if he walked out that door not to ever think he could have another chance with her. It didn't matter to him because somehow he had a feeling that eventually he and Brooke would get back together.

He made his way to his car as fast as he could. He had sobered up quite quickly and knew that he had one more very important stop to make before he went home. During the fifteen minute drive to where he used to reside he began thinking about how he would approach Brooke once he saw her. At this point his emotions were so very unpredictable. He had to make her see how special she was to him and how being apart was a huge mistake. He knew now that she was the only woman for him for the rest of his life and that he was definitely sure about that beyond any shadow of a doubt. Now he just had to convince Brooke of that.

When he pulled in the driveway of the home he once lived in, he noticed the one light on in the bedroom he had shared with Brooke for twenty years. As he made his way up the sidewalk he began feeling like a nervous schoolboy going on his first date. He wanted to say all the right things and hold her, especially hold her. When he rang the doorbell, he heard her voice faintly asking who it was. David replied, "Brooke, it's me, David. I need to see you." It had been almost two weeks since she kicked him out and that was too long ago. He desperately had to see her.

As David made his way to the door, he could see the love of his life wiping the tears away. He quietly stood there waiting to see if she would open the door. David could see that she had been crying for a while and it broke his heart that he was the one person who made her feel this bad. She was the one he was supposed to put above all others and he had failed at that. But now he was going to make things right.

"You are the last person I want to see especially at this time of the night."

"Please, listen to what I have to say," he frantically said. "I love you with everything in me and I really didn't understand how deep my love for you really was until I lost you."

He began to break down for the first time in many years and knew living life without her wasn't worth living. As he stood there looking so very helpless he noticed that his beautiful wife, standing in her old raggedy night-gown, was motioning for him to come in. David now realized how it must feel for a person to be pardoned from a crime. His second chance was staring him in the face. God forgives me for my sins so I need to do the same for David. David put his arms around me and began crying hysterically. I knew those weren't staged tears and could feel how genuinely sorry he really was. "I love you so much Brooke and I'm a fool and I am so, so very sorry for what I did to you. Please forgive me and take me back. You are the only woman I want to spend the rest of my life with." When David quit crying we began talking and trying to work through the anger, hurt, resentment and fear that had been deep within us for so long. David knew he had to come clean about the whole affair so that the healing could begin. He admitted that he shouldn't have even started chatting with strange women in the first place and had no idea it would go as far as it did. I told him the trust had been broken and that was a very hard thing to mend. He had to understand that it was going to take time for me to heal. David was feeling more confident that there might be a slim chance that they would get back together.

Before David left, he kissed me softly on the cheek and wished me a good night. As he walked out the door I stood there watching him and said quietly to myself, one day David Anderson, we may be great again. And with that I turned the light off and climbed into my bed for a much better night sleep.

Chapter 18

Ellie and Madison knew it was time to call Brooke. A month had passed and a wedding needed to be planned for December. That meant the three girls had only a few months to do it. Madison had talked to Brooke a few times since the big fiasco, but she had started back to work and had been very busy. Brooke had softened a little and Madison knew that maybe planning a night out at Angelina's would be the perfect place to start discussing the wedding with her two best friends. Now, she knew it was going to be somewhat difficult persuading Brooke to be in the same room as Ellie, but they would eventually have to be together because they were both going to be her bridesmaids.

"Absolutely not! Madison! I can't face Ellie after what she did with my husband. I am trying to get those images of David and her out of my head and seeing her now would only sharpen those images."

"Come on Brooke. Eventually you two will have to see each other at work and then when we get together at different times to plan my wedding."

I didn't know what to say because Madison was right. Could Ellie and I sit at the same table of our favorite restaurant again? Forgive her Brooke just as you are trying to do with David I kept reminding myself. What a difficult task to do.

"Madison, I need time."

"Brooke, my wedding is in five and a half months. I don't have a lot of time. Please.......... It will be like old times. I promise," she begged. But Madison didn't realize that I wouldn't allow myself to get that close to Ellie or any woman ever again. Once bitten twice shy. That sisterhood relationship was destroyed and nothing or no one could ever revive it.

Madison never seemed to take no for an answer so she told me that she had already set a reservation for Saturday evening at 6:00 at Angelina's. Madison didn't seem to be bothered by my agitation, but did change the subject. I told her about the night David had come over begging to be back in my life and how he would be a better husband and so on. Madison was curious to know if Brooke would take him back eventually.

"So are you and David going to get back together," she slyly asked.

"I don't know Madison. What he did should be unforgivable, but my faith is telling me to forgive and try again. I am struggling with it daily and am trusting that God will be in control and things will fall into place the way they are intended."

Madison wasn't a big believer in all that faith talk, but was glad to know that her best friend was sorting through the mess and trying to move forward. Madison really understood how difficult it was for Brooke because she too had been through that fire. It was a true learning experience and Madison knew that Brooke would have to make difficult decisions in the near future about her marriage. It was good that I had someone to talk to and I began feeling a little happier. After talking for thirty minutes Madison told me she needed to get off the phone because Seth had planned a fun filled day with James and her. When we hung up I knew I needed to plan my day too.

When I pulled into the parking lot of the Little Theater downtown I became very nervous and wondered if this is what I should be pursuing. Why not? I asked myself boldly. It was time I did something different for a change and I had always wanted to be an actress. I smiled and felt a little more confident and walked up the steps hoping that this change would lift my spirit and encourage me to believe in my dream and achieve it. Right now I knew I didn't need a man to help me feel good about myself. I just needed a new start. When I entered the building I did something that I hadn't done in a long time. I smiled a big smile and it felt really good.

Ellie's life hadn't changed much in the past month. She was keeping busy with her kids and had begun seeing Dr. Williams more frequently. He was a great guy and spending time with him made Ellie happy. She had been miserable and was finally beginning to find true happiness with a single man. She hadn't talked to Brooke almost the whole summer and missed sharing life's ups and downs with her. Madison was keeping busy with James and Seth most of the summer too. Ellie wanted so badly for her friendship with Brooke to heal and wondered how Saturday night would be when she and Brooke would be facing each other for the first time in a long time.

The days seemed to fly and it was now Saturday. Three incredibly changed women were on opposite sides of town getting ready for a much needed girl's night out. This time things were totally different in the way in which they all began getting ready for the evening.

Ellie was preparing a dinner for her children, but it didn't consist of chicken nuggets and french fries. Dr. Williams had introduced her to better foods to prepare for her children. This time she was making grilled chicken, brown rice and broccoli for them. She wasn't daydreaming and her thoughts were more organized. She started yoga and it was really helping her learn how to think and act in a much calmer manner. Life had changed for her and she had learned that you should never take anyone for granted. After Ellie's children ate their meal she made her way up the stairs. This time she didn't have to drag herself and reminisce about a husband that had left her. She was in better shape and when she looked into her clean bedroom she felt proud that she had been raising two wonderful children on her own and she was making it without depending on a man. Ellie's life was good right now and she thought if Brooke would forgive her life would be perfect.

Madison was enjoying the peace and quiet. Seth had taken James on a fishing excursion and this gave Madison a day to herself. She looked forward to the evening even though she was a little nervous about Brooke and Ellie seeing each other again. But Madison had a good feeling about the three of them. They had always been very close and she felt like this one incidence was just a mere roadblock. As she combed through her long, auburn hair she thought about how much life had not only changed for her, but for her two best friends as well. We are going to be just fine she said to her reflection in the mirror.

My evening was not how it had been in the past. I didn't have David admiring me from afar as I got ready for my night out. I missed him greatly, but wasn't quite ready for a truce. The separation had actually helped me lose about fifteen pounds and I was looking good. This time I decided to wear a dress instead of pants and I was feeling a little more confident with my new body. I really didn't want to attend this dinner for the fact that I would be facing the enemy, but Madison was counting on me and I didn't want to let her down. While brushing through my hair I noticed a few more gray hairs. Ugh! Didn't I have enough of those? I put my brush down and began to feel a little sad. David and I were supposed to grow old together and we were going to lift each other's spirits when the age began taking a hold on us. Where was he? I couldn't help but to think that I too had been responsible for my husband straying. For the past month I had be placing all the blame on him when really it takes two for a relationship to work. Maybe with time my heart will find a special place for him once again.

Angelina's was packed. Their reputation was growing and they seemed to be the talk of the town lately. When I arrived Ellie and Madison were sitting at the bar. It was going to be awkward, but I was going to try my best to be nice and well mannered. Ellie gave me a shy grin and Madison beckoned for me to come over. Ok, here goes I whispered. My legs felt weak and I was hoping to God that the look of hate wasn't showing on my face. I had already taken an acting class so I decided to use what I learned and it was working. When I finally made my way through the crowd I said hello to Madison and then to Ellie. Ellie stood up, walked toward me with open arms and began to cry. What was I to do? I loved this girl like she was my own sister and I had missed her so much. I didn't have to put on an act and I did what came natural. I embraced her and began to cry too. All the horrible feelings of jealousy and hate had left me miraculously and I didn't care where they had gone and hoped they would never come back. This is how it was meant to be.

Madison stood there grinning and joined us in our hug. She was making comments about how the Three Musketeers were going to be together again and we all began to laugh. We hadn't even noticed that our beeper had been flashing to let us know our table was ready. When we sat down at our corner booth, Madison told us that it was now time to get down to business and plan a wedding. I said, "First let's order our Belinis." The evening had been a success for all of us. Ellie and I were on the path to healing and Madison seemed elated with the plans that we had talked about for her wedding. Life was good and peace was among us. True friendship could withstand any of life's pitfalls. Three beautiful women had been changed forever.

Chapter 19

The alarm went off and it was dark and cold. 5:00 was the time shown on the alarm clock. What? Why is the alarm set for 5? Why is it cold in here and why is it still dark outside? I felt a warm body next to me and I jumped. "DAVID!!!!!" I screamed. It was in fact David and he was putting his arms around me. "Brooke, I love you babe, but it's time for you to get ready for work." I was so confused. Why was he in my bed? I jumped up, turned on the light, looked in the mirror and noticed I wasn't thinner. It couldn't have been summer break and my husband was by my side. As I sat there in total confusion, I rubbed my eyes and soon began to realize that what seemed to have been so real was only just a dream.

I crawled back into my warm bed, put my arms around my true love and began to cry. He asked me what was wrong, but before I could tell him I made him promise me that he would never be unfaithful and especially not with my best friend. He chuckled and said, "That must have been one hell of a dream!" I replied, "Yes it was, but thank God it was only a dream!"

THE END

Made in the USA
Lexington, KY
01 August 2012